THE PACKAGE

THE
PACKAGE

a novel

RAFAEL SILVA

LIMBIC
PRESS

Published by Limbic Press
Portland, Oregon, USA
infodesk@limbicpress.com

ISBN 978-0-991-28673-7 (paperback)
ISBN 978-0-991-28672-0 (e-book)

Library of Congress Control Number: 2019944209

Edited by Sarah Cypher
Copyediting by Jennifer Zaczek
Proofreading by Laura Whittemore
Cover and interior design by Lance Buckley
Interior photograph by Kichigin (Shutterstock Inc.)

Printed in the USA
Second Edition

To my mother and siblings, whom I love dearly.

To our cat, Fifi, who kept me company in a time of need and with whom we share a special bond.

Most of all, to my wife, whose everlasting patience, support, and love make my life possible.

…he could not avoid seeing the garden, in all its beauty, directly below him. He had not given it much thought for a few years now, until a different kind of rose caught his eye that day.

—THE PACKAGE

THE PACKAGE

PROLOGUE

I have been a secretary in this department for as long as I can remember. I have seen, heard, and accordingly gossiped about surgeons' lives since the first day I marched in here thinking I might be able to marry one of them. Thank goodness I found my Frank before complicating my life with a surgeon.

Frank was a pharmaceutical representative who often passed through the office with drug samples, pitches, and freebies for the docs. After more than thirty years, I am still going home to him completely hooked on whatever love potion he slipped into my coffee back then. But hey, that's a different story. As I was saying, since my first day of work here, I have gotten to know many people who wield scalpels for a living and who, with startling frequency, manage to slice up their own lives.

You have, for example, the gray-haired professors, with their dictatorial aura. These are the bosses. Surgery professors are always department heads and lead all medical and nonmedical hierarchies of the hospital and the medical school. Nothing gets done without their approval or their knowing about it. Really, I mean everything—including how and who will perform the most cutting-edge medical procedure, who will be admitted to the surgery program or the medical school, which secretary or janitorial staff to hire, and even what kind of pencils the department will buy. You name it, they have a say in all aspects of life here.

Consequently, they have no other life. Just look at their personal relationships. Maybe I exaggerate, but in all these years, almost every surgeon I know has been married more than once. I have spoken to their wives, girlfriends, kids, parents, and even patients more than they ever have or ever will. I have even coached some of their wives through childbirth. You laugh, but I helped pick half of their children's names.

I am not really proud of this, but more times than I care to count, I have lied for them. Sometimes these are simple white lies such as sending cards or presents on their behalf when they forget a birthday or an anniversary. Other times, my cover-ups are not that simple. For instance, they occasionally go home late or don't leave the hospital at all. When their loved ones call me to inquire about them, I provide a version of my standard answer: that they are in a long or unexpected surgical procedure. Generally, this is the truth. But sometimes, the real answer involves them "working" with the right young nurse or colleague. There is always someone who is more than willing to "help" take care of their needs during the countless hours they spend within the walls of this institution.

Things are easier with the younger docs. The food chain continues downward from the professors, also known as attendings, to the subspecialty fellows, chief residents, senior residents, junior residents, interns, and senior and junior medical students. Their lives are not much different. But it is typically easier for me to cover up their bad habits or infidelities because they are often unmarried and usually don't have children.

Is it the same for the women docs, you ask? You bet. A lot of them are the most impossible bitches, with truly chaotic lives. But I have never encountered more dedicated, strong-willed, and brilliant women than these surgeons.

Save for a select few—and I'll get to one of them in a minute—surgeons are hard to get along with. They have short fuses, bad attitudes, foul mouths, and god complexes. They are members of a profession that lives to work. Do I sound bitter? Yes and no. My first weeks in the office, I checked the classified ads every Sunday. I wanted out. Yet somehow, I learned to deal with, understand, and in due course, befriend almost all of them. I have been and continue to be like a mother to many of them. They come to me, entrust me with their problems, and often ask me for advice.

They are sort of messed up. I know it. But I love them, I respect them, and I meddle in their lives because in the end, they are all heroes.

This is the story of one of these heroes—an exception to the norm—whose fate in life and love needed a helping hand.

ONE

On a cold New Haven spring afternoon, the postman came into the office, dripping wet. I teased him, asking if he could please dry out before stepping in and soaking my carpet. He smiled and handed me the usual carton full of correspondence. After signing his electronic notepad, for a package that required signature for delivery, I sent him on his way. Once he was gone, I proceeded to open and sort the journals, invitations to medical seminars, letters from prospective young surgeons begging to enter the residency program, et cetera and placed each piece in its respective mailbox.

From time to time, some of the correspondence could be personal—from birthday cards to parking tickets to divorce papers. These matters, too, went through me because the doctors generally lacked the time and proclivity to deal with them. So, I often took it upon myself to analyze their personal mail and make decisions or take actions as necessary.

The last thing in the carton that day was a rectangular box wrapped in generic shipping paper, secured with twine, and addressed to Dr. Declan Baltierra. This was the package that had required signature upon delivery. It was a bit heavy. Its size and shape suggested a bottle of liquor or the like. This was not unusual, as many of Dr. Baltierra's former patients often sent wine or other kinds of alcohol as gifts to express their gratitude. These gifts ranged from the ordinary to the unique and insanely expensive. I thought about placing it intact on his desk. But curiosity got the best of me, and I decided to open it. After cutting the twine's bowknot, I carefully removed the thick paper and then the bubble wrap. Underneath, I encountered a case made of shiny mahogany. *Not a cheap drink*, I thought. I unlatched the lock, which seemed to be real gold, and opened the lid.

It was not a bottle. If the object before my eyes was real, I could not believe it. I sat there and stared at it for what seemed like an eternity. Then it all made sense. There was a note in meticulous handwriting inside the box:

To my Angel of Independence,

Please add this trophy to the countless others you must surely have. It is legitimately yours.

Thank you.

No signature, no indication of the sender's identity. I later realized that if I had examined the contents further, I would have known who'd sent it. But even then, I had a hunch regarding its origin.

You know, some research shows that parents often have a favorite child. This made me feel better. Of all the young men and women under my motherly wing, Declan was my favorite. He was a young surgeon who trained in cardiothoracic surgery in Texas and whose intellectual and technical gifts made him, at thirty-three, the most sought-after man in the world of academic surgery. Toward the end of his surgical training, he considered job offers from the most prestigious institutions in the country. Perhaps because he'd gone to Yale as an undergraduate, he decided to accept the faculty position here, at the Yale School of Medicine. He'd been with us for over three years. I've never met another surgeon—or, frankly, another person quite like him. Needless to say, regarding the package, I took affairs into my own hands and stuck my nose deep into somebody else's life.

I closed the box and fumbled around for the return shipping address. The postal service does not deliver packages without one. I looked at Declan's schedule for the next few weeks, broke out some new hospital letterhead, and I simply wrote a date, time, place, and seat number and signed it: *Trust me, your and his best friend.* Then I added a small footnote: *P.S. Consider the Omni Hotel at Yale.* I stuffed the brief letter in an institutional envelope, addressed it to "the resident of," and ran down to the post office to make it all happen. Just as I dropped it in the mail slot, I got a bit nervous for a second. Then I thought, *What's done is done, and chances are, nothing bad will come of it.* At the end of the day, I took the package home to tell my Frank all about it.

He was retired now. He had climbed the company ladder in his salesman days, and we lived comfortably in a beautiful house near Science Hill. We had one kid, Frank Jr., who was a great radiologist and a very happy family man out in California. Tea was already waiting for me when I arrived home. I placed the box on the kitchen table and took off my cold-weather gear.

"Hey, Iris, what's this?" Frank asked.

"It's an unfinished story."

"Oh crap. Oh no. You are not meddling again, are you? Who is it now? What is this?" Frank proceeded to open the box in his curious and customary way. He looked at the contents and then glanced at me with incredulous eyes. "Hon?"

"Give me that! If you must know, I think it's the real thing. Like I said, it's an unfinished—ah, situation."

"Honey, the last time you had a situation at work, we had three different women and one truly deranged kid receiving therapy from us. Please, tell me it's not about any of your surgeons."

"Well, it is. Besides, it's about Declan. You know how much I like him. He is different. I think he deserves the plan I've put in motion for him. That is, of course, if it works out."

"Declan? Tell me again about him." Frank settled into his chair at the table and lined up our tea mugs.

Once comfortable, we sat in the twilight of the evening with Rif, our Labrador, and I told Frank Declan's story—a story in which the package might just play an important role.

TWO

I t was a night of debauchery and sin in Galveston, Texas.

A swarm of young adults from the Houston area had descended on the island to consume the truckloads of alcohol that had been wheeled in for Mardi Gras. The Strand District sparkled with glitter as bands and floats paraded down its streets, with participants throwing colorful beads at thousands of inebriated spectators. The bars and dance halls conveniently forgot their fire marshal capacity codes and bustled to serve the sea of customers. Jazz music and tobacco smoke emanated from the open windows of every business along the parade route.

Meanwhile, in operating room 26 at the nearby University of Texas Medical Branch, heart surgeons were working on a tedious heart-lung transplant. OR 16 had a nineteen-year-old kid who was reportedly minding his own business a few hours earlier and had been shot in the chest by "a bullet that came out of nowhere." And in OR 4, Declan was helping neurosurgeons cut out some kind of spine infection that had to be approached through the chest. He had just finished his general surgery residency eleven months ago and had joined the cardiothoracic team as a fellow. This meant he was about two years away from being a bona fide heart surgeon. At any rate, the chest surgery staff had their hands full.

Around one in the morning, Declan was done clearing the heart and lungs. It was time for the neurosurgeons to work their magic. He stepped back, sat on a stool, and caught some "standing sleep." That's what the surgeons call it. They never really sleep during their long shifts. As they say, "You catch sleep if and when you can." A few minutes went by, and his pager went off. Since he was still scrubbed in, the OR nurse checked the page and called the number.

"Dr. Baltierra, it's Dr. Williams from the emergency room. He wants to know if you could please look at some X-rays with him."

"What do you think, Patty?" Declan replied, raising his gloved hands.

She turned back to the phone. "I'm sorry, Dr. Williams, he is scrubbed in at the moment." There was a pause, after which Patty simply said, "Okay, bye."

Shortly after the phone call, Dr. Williams himself appeared in the OR, gowned and holding a set of films.

When Declan saw them, he exclaimed, "Oh shit! Still alive?"

"Yeah, man, she's drunk and high out of her mind. Anesthesia and Medicine are up there trying to decide what to give her to slow her down."

"We have to show these to Dr. Katz." Declan leaned closer to the image showing a severely injured aorta. "Damn, I just don't know how we're gonna deal with this."

"I know you guys are spread out really thin tonight. Should we fly her back to Houston?" Dr. Williams asked.

"No, she'd probably die on the way there. Hold on."

Declan asked the neuro guys if they were okay. They gave him a simple "uh-hum" without looking up. Declan broke out of his gown and went to OR 26 to explain the situation and check on a plan of action with the boss.

Dr. Katz was sixty-something, tall, and stern. He'd been working on a heart-lung transplant for nearly three hours straight. He was not about to be pulled from such a delicate procedure. But he took a moment to review the films and said, "It looks bad. Wake up Tom Montgomery and bring him in." When the nurse didn't move fast enough, he added, "And I mean yesterday." Then he told Declan, "Make sure you keep her alive. If she crashes, well, it's all you, Dec. Can you handle it?" He looked at Declan over his surgical mask with a set of gray, piercing eyes.

"Of course," Declan replied. Under the circumstances, this was any surgeon's standard answer.

Declan burst out of that room and went into the suite with the gunshot wound case. He asked the attending surgeon, who was also too busy to help, if he would occasionally look in and help the neuro guys. Declan got a positive nod. Along with Dr. Williams, he rushed to the ER to check on the patient in question. The anesthesiologist had finally sedated her. She was now on a gurney, sleeping.

—m—

"Hey, how do you know this? What does this have to do with the package?" Frank shook his head. "Honey, please don't embellish the story. Just tell me what this is all about. You've never even been to Texas."

"Shut up, Frank. I am telling you exactly the way it is and how this box came to lie on our kitchen table. Besides, you surely enjoy a detailed story. I know things because my docs talk to me. A lot of Declan's story I got one afternoon when you were on a fishing trip. I invited him over for lunch after one of his lectures on Science Hill. So, sit there, shut your hole, and listen. Pass me the sugar. Anyway, before I was so rudely interrupted, the story is that this girl—"

"When you say 'girl,' you don't mean…?" Frank pointed to the mahogany box on the table.

"Well, I think so." And again I asked him to stop interrupting so I could continue telling him Declan's story.

—m—

The girl was, well, troubled—emotionally and socially. You know, into drugs and all kinds of questionable endeavors. She had apparently been having a routine night out with a group of friends when they decided to drive down from Houston to join the decadence in Galveston. They didn't make it far. Just outside the Clear Lake city limits, they plowed into the side of a big rig. Half of them went to a hospital there, and two, including this girl, were airlifted to the trauma center in Galveston.

Now she lay in a trauma bay, disheveled and reeking of alcohol. A catheter hung from her bladder, tubes protruded from both sides of her chest, and streaks of dried blood covered her body. Her lips and eyelids were painted black. Gunk was visible under her nails. Parts of her skin were cracked and blemished. Her multicolored hair was stiff and greasy. Metal rings pierced various body parts, but despite these decorations, she had a semblance of personal neglect.

When Declan arrived to examine her, two medical students were at her sides, cleaning up her wounds and looking for one deep enough to practice suturing. He stood at the foot of the stretcher for a minute before he placed a hand on her. In turn, members of the trauma team stared at him, hoping he would make a decision about the patient and allow them to go back to sleep.

After a brief physical exam, he looked at the medical students and said, "Carry on, guys." Then, to the chief resident in charge of Trauma Team One, he said, "Hey, Brian, if I go to the OR with this one, I will need you. So, you can send the rest of the team to sleep. Let your attending know, and share the love with Team Two—they are now first call for the night."

Soon, Declan was on the phone with Dr. Montgomery, who was caught on the mainland trying to get across the causeway to the island. Declan described the patient to him as a twenty-four-year-old, heavily intoxicated woman who had been involved in a motor vehicle accident and had suffered several fractures, small lacerations to the extremities, bilateral pneumothoraces, and blunt trauma to the chest. Radiology studies, among other things, showed evidence of an aortic injury. And that yes, she was still alive and presently stable. Declan was ordered to prepare a cardiac surgery suite and round up a couple of general surgery residents, which he had already done.

As Dec sat in the emergency room waiting for Dr. Montgomery to arrive and finish the preparations, he felt an abysmal uncertainty. He knew the patient was facing an uphill battle. His superior was stuck in impenetrable traffic, and his patient was one of the two out of a hundred people with a ruptured aorta who arrive at a hospital alive.

I can't let someone so young die, he thought.

During the physical exam, his thoughts had briefly wandered beyond medical technicalities. A singular uneasiness enveloped him in the minute or so he'd stood at the bedside observing the patient. *How could someone so beautiful wear this mask?* he'd wondered.

When Declan looked at this patient, he was able to see beyond her appearance. He was caught off guard by an ambivalence of feelings that swayed from a detached doctor-patient relationship to something more—a rush of feelings he had never previously experienced when assessing a patient.

As Declan was still trying to make sense of his emotions, one of the medical students burst out of the trauma bay and shouted urgently that the patient's breathing and tracings on the monitor didn't look right.

She was crashing.

THREE

"Let's get some blood going, now."

"LR wide open! Somebody, crash cart."

"Tube her!"

"Hey, people, be careful with those chest tubes. X-ray, stat."

"What's the BP?"

"Can't get it, Doc. I'll do a manual."

Declan yelled from behind the crowd, "Is the OR ready?"

No answer.

"BP, fifty over palp."

"Still with us!"

Residents and emergency-room attending physicians were doing most of the work. It was a typical scene of controlled chaos. Declan was just far enough from the center of activity to allow the others to do their job. He saw the two medical students along the far wall observing and analyzing everything before them—the action they were training for. They surely felt helpless and, like all medical students at times like this, probably wondered whether they would be able to handle a similar situation in just a few years. Everyone around that young woman was intoxicated with adrenaline.

Declan looked at her face and was arrested by a glimpse of her eyes. She was not quite conscious, but there was something inexplicably magical about their eyes meeting. It was instantaneous but felt without end. Was it the look of helplessness and pleading for one's life? Maybe. Declan knew her case was grim at best. Then, slowly, her eyes closed again, and a sparkling tear ran, as if in slow motion, down her cheek. It glittered in the light, continued downward, and sank deep in his heart.

"No pulse! Monitor?"

"V-fib!"

"Okay, charge paddles!"

"No, wait." It was Dr. Williams who asked everybody to "stop and chill out for a second!" Then he turned to Declan with an inquiring face.

Declan took a deep breath, closed his eyes momentarily, and in a stern voice declared, "Okay, people, I need the thoracotomy tray, two guys who want to go all the way, and somebody to push us to the operating room because we are going *now.*"

Declan split the side of her chest open right then and there. He contained the bleeding and had his guys take turns on their way to the OR doing compressions on her heart.

Eventually, of course, he had to crack open the middle of her chest, but I just don't know the details of what else Declan did in the OR. Dr. Montgomery didn't make it into the hospital until much later, when Declan had already fixed a very big problem. When asked if he wanted any help closing up the details, Dec politely declined. So, Montgomery told him he'd be in a bedroom sleeping and to feel free to call him for help.

"More tea?" Frank asked.

"Sure. Thank you," I said, and I continued with the story.

No surgeon ever took the time to close up a chest as carefully as Declan did. The nurses noticed.

"Pretty girl, huh, Dr. Bal?"

"Yeah, I just hope she makes it without permanent brain or heart damage."

"Hey, if I ever need cuttin', I want you to do it. With those stitches, she may even wear a cute bikini someday." There was a brief moment of silence. "Just trying to butter you up, Dr. Bal. You are doing a good thing, and we all love you for it."

"Thanks, Nancy. Now, could we get some tunes going?"

"Right away."

He finished his work to the voice of Andrea Bocelli's interpretation of "Che gelida manina" from *La Bohème.*

After more than thirty hours on his feet, Declan caught forty minutes of solid sleep. Then it was time for morning rounds. He saw his other patients; rounded with Dr. Katz, who matter-of-factly told him he had done a "fine job on the ruptured girl"; and then grabbed a bite to eat. Declan had a full day ahead of him: two conferences, a medical student lecture, clinic, and a coronary bypass that Dr. Montgomery couldn't do because he had gotten behind and had to catch a plane to somewhere.

It was six p.m. when he finally had a chance to eat his second meal of the day. He joined some of his team members in the break room for a typical round of trash-talk and sandwiches.

"Sorry to leave you clowns, but I have to check on my case from last night," Declan said after a short while.

"That punk girl? Don't worry, dude. I saw her this afternoon, pretty SNAFU," his senior resident said. Then, reflexively and in a sarcastic monotone, the whole gang repeated in unison: "Situation Normal, All Fucked Up!" Everyone laughed.

"Go home and crash," said another one of his buddies, to which Declan replied, "Ten-four, man." He felt a bit disappointed not checking on the patient himself, but he grabbed his coat and walked out to his bike. On the short ride home, he tried to go over the events of the past forty-eight hours. He could only think of that girl. He had saved her life but placed an enormous question mark on her future and on her chances of ever regaining normal function. Declan wished he could know if there was any significant brain damage. If it was extensive, it may have been better to let her die in the first place. He was conflicted—as all physicians are when they hold in their hands the power to affect the balance between life and death.

Dammit, what was her name? Declan thought as he shut his apartment door behind him.

Given his focus on the complex technicalities of her case the previous night, he never quite came across her name.

FOUR

It was still dark the next morning when Declan's bike followed the same path but in the opposite direction. At a distance, he could discern sounds of the eternal altercations between the water of the Gulf and the Galveston shore. Seagulls flew around the athletic field to his right, and a subtle drizzle serenely filled the air. As he made a turn into the main hospital complex, the tranquility of the previous few minutes vanished, turning abruptly into a less ethereal rush of adrenaline and a call to focus on the more tangible intricacies of the work ahead. A reality check waited just beyond the automatic sliding doors. When the doors opened, a flurry of cold air hit him in the face and immediately brought to mind the long list of patients in his care.

One of the few perks of being a fellow was that, except for attending surgeons, Declan was in command. This meant that his team would have pre-rounded before he got in. They would have seen all of the team's patients and gathered all pertinent information, from laboratory results and X-rays to admission and discharge paperwork. The usual suspects on his team included a fourth-year surgery resident named Henry, a third-year named John, an intern everyone called Tiny, and two new third-year medical students. Rounds always started with the sickest patients, so he met his team in the surgical intensive care unit.

"Hey, Henry, what's up?"

"Not much, Dec, just hangin' out. Listen, John is upstairs finishing up the floor patients, and Tiny is showing the new students around."

"On Saturday? I thought the student rotation started Monday."

"Yeah, but it's their first month of surgery, and they are scared shitless. They want to get a head start and learn the patients. I think they're gonna be pretty good. It's a guy and a girl."

"She cute?" Declan joked.

"Believe you me, she'll make our days this month a whole lot brighter," Henry said, smiling.

"What is the story on Ramos here?" Dec pointed to the chart outside the first patient's room.

"He went to angio yesterday. Our repair is fine. Turns out he had a GI bleed. They pumped some Pitressin, and it looks like the guy can get out of the unit today. Incision is okay. He got one unit of packed cells yesterday and feels well. Of course, until he finds he has colon cancer or something bad in his gut," Henry said, only half joking.

"Yeah, wouldn't that suck? But we'll leave that for someone else to deal with down the road." Dec shook his head sincerely.

"Next is Finkle. Status-post-CABG. Pain controlled. Vitals stable. Ticking strong. Labs okay. Moderate effusion. We'll get another chest film this afternoon, and if it improves, we'll think about kicking him out too. I figured we could start him back on his old meds."

"Fine," Declan said.

One after another, they saw a total of six patients. They checked wounds, started and ended medications, stopped and ordered laboratory and imaging studies, and so on. Then they went to see their last unit patient, who happened to be on their list as a consult. The trauma team was primarily responsible for her care. Tiny and the students were at her bedside.

"And as promised, here is da man behind the story I just told you," Tiny said. "His name is Dr. Baltierra, and you will refer to him as Dec, lest you make him feel old and have that adversely affect your evaluations at the end of this month's extravaganza. Dec, allow me to introduce my two new servants—I mean students—Abby and Mike. I told them they were crazy showing up on a Saturday morning, but they were already here. So, I showed them around and gave them the scoop."

"Well, don't believe anything this guy says," Declan said. "He has a broad imagination and forgets he has only been a doctor for a few months."

"Dude, I almost had them idolizing me for the last hour. Now they'll lose all respect," Tiny retorted in jest.

"Despite what the illustrious Dr. Tiny may have told you, you guys should really take a load off. I know you are a bit nervous. But we'll try to help you in any way we can. All we ask is that you are always on time, especially on OR days. Be prepared, and know your patients. You will find that we often nickname and joke a bit about everybody, even our patients. It's all in good spirit, to blow off steam. In the end, we respect the patients and give all of them the best care possible. Anyway, that's as much administrative stuff as I want to say. How is this one doing?" Declan asked.

Tiny presented the patient.

"Miss Madison came in Thursday night with multiple injuries, mostly ortho and of no interest to us. Relevant, however, is her ruptured pseudoaneurysm of the aorta, status-post interposition graft repair by Dec here. She is still vented and unresponsive. Vitals are tachy but otherwise stable. All pulses are strong and equal. Incision looks good. There are two chest tubes in place, but Trauma is taking care of them. The plan is to sit on her for a couple of days and maybe repeat an angio. We will continue the present med regimen and keep following pressures."

Henry cut in, "Tiny here is a good man and basically told us what we needed to know, but for your benefit," he told the medical students, "we will expect you guys to give more detailed and organized presentations during rounds. Okay, everyone seems tucked in here, so let's go see how John is doing upstairs."

Declan was quiet and thoughtful as he led the group out. Once in the elevator, he matter-of-factly asked, "Hey, that girl, what was her name again?"

"Madison. Lauren Madison," Abby said.

FIVE

By midmorning, Declan and the rest of the gang packed themselves into Abby's convertible VW Cabriolet and headed to La Estacion, a hole-in-the-wall type of establishment just off the Strand. Mexican hats, colorful serapes, and neon beer emblems hung precariously all over the sixties-era wood paneling. The corner opposite the entrance was a nebula of smoke into which waitresses seemed to disappear momentarily only to emerge with trays full of the most popular breakfast in town. The clientele was a fairly even mix of townsfolk and those associated with the medical center. Behind the charismatic cashier, who perpetually signaled the waitresses to fill empty coffee cups and iced tea glasses, was a wall awash in postcards from all over the US and the world. The postcards were addressed to various members of the wait- or kitchen staff. Most were from former med students and residents, whose careers now lay far from the island but who remained thankful for the countless tacos that fueled them throughout their medical training.

The conversation initially revolved around the students, because it's so easy to start by asking what specialty they plan on going into.

Traditionally, to kiss up, the answer is always the specialty you are presently rotating through. If the answer is pediatrics while doing internal medicine, for example, the consensus is that your boss assumes your level of interest is low. Consequently, you may get pushed aside, even ignored, and the lack of attention could have a negative impact on the ever-important final evaluation. Of course, this is mostly an archaic custom of medical school that in no way should affect a student's participation on the team.

"S-surgery," Abby and Mike answered, almost in unison.

"Well, you guys landed on the right team," John said as he sprayed his fifth lemon wedge on a steaming bowl of menudo. He was one of very few folks who, outside of the Mexican community, truly enjoyed a dish with cow gut as the main ingredient.

"We've said this before, but as long as shit gets done, we won't keep you guys working unnecessarily or make your lives impossible. You are probably coming in thinking your lives will be hell for the next month. Forget it. Your job is to learn. The worst thing that happens on this team is that patients die, and, well, that is Dec's responsibility." Henry smiled and lifted an eyebrow toward Dec.

"Yeah, but that doesn't mean what you do is not important," Declan said. "My name, Henry's, and the attending's may top the chart after a long procedure, but your sore muscles and sweat will go into holding those retractors. The team is all seven of us. That is, us plus Dr. Katz, who you will rarely see. We'll look after and help each other this month, okay?"

Then, just before downing a forkful of bacon and potatoes, Tiny said, "Unlike some of your buddies on other surgical teams, the sphincters in this group are nice and relaxed. So, you can tell us what you are *really* going into."

Abby and Mike looked at each other for a second and were unable to hold back a pair of frank smiles.

"I am actually thinking about radiology," Mike said.

"Uh-huh, you must be a smart guy," Henry replied. "We'll see about that."

Then everyone turned to Abby.

"I don't think you guys really want to know…" There was an expectant pause. "Okay, psych," she said finally.

They looked at each other with furrowed foreheads, lopsided grins, and raised eyebrows. Then Tiny broke the silence.

"Yeah, you have that Hollywood-type, classy-babe look that can shrink all kinds of brains." Then, driving a fork through the yolk of his remaining sunny-side up, he added, "And I mean that in a good, non-sexually-harassing sort of way."

They all cracked up.

Over the next thirty minutes, they all found out more about one another. Abby was from Houston but had gone to college at Stanford. Mike was from El Paso, went to UT San Antonio, and both his parents were cardiologists. Henry and John were married and were die-hard UT Austin Longhorns. Tiny's real name was Leighton. He was an A&M Aggie from East Texas who grew up listening to his father tell him that his "fat ass will never amount to nothin'." He was now far removed from home and lived for surgery, food, and his monthly column in *Fat and Proud Magazine*. Declan was born in Laredo, Texas, to a Mexican father and an Irish mother. He grew up in Mexico City, had gone to Yale, and had done all of his medical training in Galveston.

With bellies full and bills paid, Declan turned to Abby and said, "Why don't you take us back to campus so we can all go home and do something productive with the rest of the day."

"Yeah, I got craploads of laundry to do," John said.

Henry reached for one of the complimentary mint candies in a basket on the counter as they exited the restaurant. "Dude, I thought your mom did that shit for you."

"Fuck you, man," John replied.

As Abby pulled up to the main hospital complex, Declan told the students, "I'll see you two gunners on Monday. The rest of you boys, same time and place for rounds tomorrow." Everyone got out of the car except Tiny, who asked Abby for a ride to the AKK house. This was one of the medical student fraternities at UTMB, where he had lived while in med school and where he planned to stay for as long as possible. During the interim ride, Tiny again reassured Abby that as long as Declan was in charge, their rotation would be enjoyable. When they arrived and Tiny was getting out of the car, Abby hesitantly asked him whether Declan was married.

"Nope," he answered.

"Oh. Well, see ya Monday, Tiny." She pressed on the gas pedal and slowly pulled away.

"Take care," Tiny said. He waved and simultaneously thought, *Wow, this is gonna be interesting.*

SIX

Mondays sucked.

The team barely had time to buy lunch after morning rounds and case conference. They methodically dispersed as they exited the elevator and went through the cafeteria's west entrance. Henry and Mike opted for ready-made sandwiches, several pieces of assorted fruit, and popcorn. John and Abby went for a meat-lover's special and a vegetable burrito from the Pizza Hut/Taco Bell counter. At John's advice, Abby jammed her pockets full of saltine crackers. "For later, you know," he said. Tiny dragged a full five minutes behind, as he chose a combination of all his team's lunch items.

They exited the cafeteria's east door and, in an almost military fashion, proceeded to the stairs with their hands full of food. This intentionally longer route led up three flights into the Children's Hospital, right into the gynecology offices, left through radiology, and up five more flights, giving them about ten minutes to eat their meal before reaching the dreaded outpatient clinic building. Everyone dropped the last bits of their main food items either in the trashcan just outside the surgery clinic or, if seasoned and smart enough, down their throats. They took a few properly concealed snacks into the clinic with them.

Surgeons, as a matter of tradition, always wore clothes worthy of a tie under their white coats during morning rounds and, above all, during clinic. While nonsurgical staff members strutted around wearing scrubs all the time, a surgeon wore them only in the operating room. Furthermore, as grave a sin as it was to wear scrubs to clinic, it was even worse to bring in food.

When the gang arrived, Declan had already seen four of the day's thirty-five scheduled patients. As soon as his eyes connected with his team, he took off his coat, hung it strategically on the only chair in the exam room corridor, and in his off-green scrub top, walked out the door. This was a prearranged plan in which crackers, energy bars, and a few other goodies were dumped in Dec's four coat pockets for all of them to share throughout the long day. With the team starting to take over things, Declan strolled toward the clinic offices to retrieve radiology reports. As he passed Tiny in the hallway, there was a sneaky transfer of contraband—two Taco Supremes—that Tiny had procured for him.

Despite occasional accusatory glances from superiors, the chief wore scrubs and no coat. The troops smuggled in food, which they periodically ate while seeing patients, out of sight from the powers that be. These little subversions may have seemed petty and insignificant, but they made the long days bearable.

It was around six in the evening when the last patient left. The team had dealt with everything from patients' physical and psychological issues to procuring some of them a taxi ride home. For their first clinic day, Mike and Abby shadowed the crew. Well, more specifically, Mike took turns seeing patients with Tiny, John, and Henry, while Abby worked with Dec most of the time. Henry told a seventy-year-old woman that her quadruple bypass was a success and that as long as she took her medications and moderately adhered to the specified diet and exercise plan, she would not need the services of a heart surgeon for at least ten more years. Tiny got stuck with a fifty-two-year-old man whose fear of an anticipated heart valve operation kept him crying inconsolably throughout the pre-op interview and physical exam. Dec told a young man and his family that his team would likely be successful in removing a cancerous tumor from his heart but that his prognosis and treatment would then be in the hands of the oncologists. John was attacked by a man whose persistent indulgence in Jack Daniel's and Camel Lights would give him zero chance at receiving a heart transplant. In between the psychological and administrative roller coaster, they all changed bandages, removed sutures, prescribed medications, and grappled with their own emotions.

At the end of clinic, Declan put on his coat, its pockets now empty. Then he and his team strolled down to the cafeteria. They shared stories and dinner before gathering again in the ICU for evening rounds. Dec checked out by phone with Dr. Katz, and their day was done just after seven p.m.

"I'm going to do some weights. Anyone?" John asked.

"Are you stupid or something?" Tiny retorted.

"Pass," Henry said.

"Abby? Mike?" John turned his head back and forth between them.

"John is reaching. Someone! Please, go work out with the guy," Tiny pleaded.

Abby shrugged. "As much as I would love to join you, the only weights I use at the gym are light dumbbells. I would be a lousy spot at the bench. Jogging is my thing, so you are welcome to come out to the track with me."

"No, thanks. Running is too cardiovascular for me. I'm more sedentary, so I stick to weights," John said. "I'm sure you can run with Dec, though. Barring a surgical procedure, he runs on the beach every day, rain or shine. Ain't that true, captain?"

"You bet," Dec answered.

Finally, Mike agreed to work out with John. "I was going to shoot some hoops, but it's too dark out anyway. I'll go pump some iron with you, man."

They all stopped at the bike rack just outside, and Declan told them to try to get some rest. Then, specifically to John, he said, "You are with me on the tumor guy tomorrow. Make sure you also lift the anatomy textbook sometime tonight."

"So, Dec, how far do you go?" Abby asked once he'd pulled his bike off the rack. The rest of the team had dispersed.

"Oh, from Casa Caribe to the island's north end and back. It's about a three-mile run. Short, nice, and effective."

"Do you go fast?"

— ⁓ —

Abby and Declan had agreed to meet that night for a run. They started their jog in front of his apartment on First Street and headed to the beach. Moonlight shone on the sand at the edge of the water. Lights flickered from the distant oil rigs. The breeze was refreshing, and the sound of breaking waves accompanied the rhythm of their breaths. Their brief spurts of conversation were amenable.

Abby, however, realized that Dec did not "go fast" at all.

SEVEN

Things were status quo for the ensuing week. Work was efficient and, thanks to the team's minor operating procedure rebellions on clinic days, relatively enjoyable. Abby and Mike were already suturing up saphenous vein incisions on bypass patients. Everyone else gradually shouldered more responsibility in and out of the OR. On more than one occasion, their teamwork was praised by the revered yet mostly absent Dr. Katz.

They also bonded outside the hospital. Mike and Henry convinced John to lay off the weights and Tiny to lay off the late-night snacks. The four of them alternated nights shooting hoops and shooting pool, and sometimes Henry's and John's wives came along. Declan and Abby were still running together almost every day. Abby was an extremely attractive woman. And Declan was not stupid. Both felt a definite chemistry. But Declan kept their conversations strictly platonic. As long as Abby was his medical student, anything beyond work and friendly exercise would be inappropriate. Except for the occasional, almost imperceptible flirt, Abby had not pushed.

The following week, a series of explosions at a nearby Texas City refinery changed everything. Dozens of workers lost their lives, and dozens of others were severely injured. A level-one disaster protocol went into effect, and all resident and attending surgeons were called into action. It was an apocalyptic scene. Helicopters from UTMB, Houston hospitals, and the Coast Guard circled above the trauma center as they took turns delivering wounded workers. The parade of ambulances on the street was organized chaos.

Ortho and Plastics were busy with limb traumas and burns. The rest of the surgical subspecialty teams went back to being general surgeons and took care of other injuries. Declan, Henry, and John operated on a case of internal bleeding and one case of complete evisceration—a man whose intestines were hanging out from a gaping wound in his abdomen. Tiny, Mike, and Abby dealt with less complicated cases: removal of superficial foreign bodies, minor burns, and suturing.

When the dust settled the next morning, nearly twenty major trauma operations had taken place, and only a handful of cases had been diverted to Houston hospitals. The entire medical staff was beyond the point of exhaustion. Despite this, they still had to handle all their routine activities. Fueled by a well-deserved sense of pride and duty, they were able to forge ahead.

As a result of these events, trauma teams were overwhelmed. They would be unable to care for all the new patients. Thus, patient rosters had to be altered, and non-trauma teams inherited the overflow. Most of the hits went to general surgery teams. After the trading and shuffling, Dec's team ended up with four new patients: the two men they operated on the previous night, one hernia repair case, and the young woman they had recently signed off their consult list. John had been following her. After the operation, Declan saw her only a couple of times and heard about her in passing. Now, Lauren was back on his service and, irrevocably, in his mind.

Lauren was out of intensive care and on the regular floor. The endotracheal and chest tubes had been removed. Mike had taken off most of the remaining bandages from her chest, shoulders, and legs. A Foley catheter, NG tube, and a right arm splint remained in place. She was still unconscious, though, and feeding was becoming a problem. While a CT scan and encephalogram showed that her brain appeared intact, the neurology team reported that her clinical exam was confusing. It was difficult to predict when she would, if at all, wake up from her coma. She had hitherto been fed through her nose via the NG tube. Now, she could basically be transferred to a skilled nursing facility but needed a PEG tube before that could happen. This contraption required making a hole through the abdomen and into the stomach. A tube with an inflatable balloon inside, which keeps the tube from falling out, would then be placed through the hole, allowing for long-term feeding.

Something over and above Dec's medical judgment made him stall. He had the ability and jurisdiction to say that her post-operative status deserved additional observation. He kept her on their patient roster. Meanwhile, to Abby's dismay, he suddenly stopped their jogging routine. After rounds, he stayed in the hospital and, in an old-fashioned, marginally unorthodox manner, began to read aloud at Lauren's bedside. The first day he read out of two back issues of *People* and an article on repairing ventricular septal defects of the heart. *If this were my mother,* he thought, *I'd be doing the same thing.*

Every other paragraph, he directed a glance at Lauren—perhaps looking for a response, perhaps just looking. She had become emaciated. She had multiple bruises all over her neck and arms from numerous blood draws and IV exchanges. Her hair was slimy. Her lips were dry and cracked. Her skin was pale and smelled of chronic disease. What on earth did he see in her?

Whatever it was brought him back again the next few evenings. On one of the nights, he prepared and rehearsed a lecture and later read to her from the *Houston Chronicle.* The door to her room was kept open. From the nursing station not too far away, staff members would point and whisper among themselves as they saw him pacing around the room and talking to the comatose girl. Instantly, that became one more of the many things they loved about him.

One night, just before he left, Dec noticed that Lauren's left hand was stuck between the mattress and the railing on the bed. So, he walked to the left side of the bed, gently dislodged her hand, and placed it on her chest. For a split yet seemingly endless second, his hand remained in contact with hers.

Once back in his apartment that night, before drifting to sleep, Declan realized that his feelings were more complicated than pity or a doctor's devotion to his patient. He could not quite sort them out. She was his patient, so what on earth was he thinking? What did he expect? *You are a prudent and respected surgeon,* he told himself. *What the hell are you doing with this woman? Damn, you are six years her senior.*

He reasoned that his feelings for Lauren, whatever else they might have been, were untimely and unbecoming. He decided he would place her on the schedule to put the PEG tube in her stomach himself and ship her out.

On Wednesday night, after about a week of reading to her each night, he could not help but go to her room one more time. He fixed his gaze on her eroded lips and whispered a final "Good luck."

Whether by chance or on purpose, Abby spotted Declan at a distance as he stood at Lauren's side. Now she knew why her running mate had bailed on her. And she confirmed what she had suspected of late. It had been about a month now since she'd joined the team. As many sensible women would, Abby had developed a crush on Declan. She was neither malicious nor a possessive person. Yet seeing him with Lauren stirred up a sense of jealousy.

Thursday and Friday were OR days. It wasn't unusual for female staff to wear nothing but a scrub top over their bras, with no shirt in between. Abby usually opted for the extra layer. Not those two days, though. She made a point to scrub in on Declan's cases. In the most understated, classy, and yet obviously flirtatious way, Abby found an excuse to stoop or move her arms so that Dec—and, unavoidably, other members of the gang—would witness her ample sex appeal. Friday was her and Mike's last day with the team, and she was determined to ask Declan out on a date.

That last Friday morning, to Abby's dismay, Tiny reported that Ms. Lauren Madison was finally out of her coma. She wasn't fully coherent and was a bit under the weather. But Neurology was swiftly trying to tune things up. However, to Abby's surprise, Dec accepted her hesitant invitation to "catch a movie or something."

—⁂—

"Wow! I guess in these cases reading aloud to somebody in a coma and flaunting one's bodily charms really works."

"Oh, Frank," I said and smiled. I actually agreed with him.

EIGHT

John presented Lauren on morning rounds that Saturday.

"Once again, twenty-four-year-old female on hospital day number twenty-nine, status-post multiple traumatic injuries, on our service by default. She did, however, have a pseudoaneurysm repair. Recently became conscious. No complaints, although not talking much. Denies pain. Vitals are stable. Nasogastric and Foley catheters in place. Intake and output okay. Lungs are a bit junky. Bowel sounds okay. She is fairly alert and oriented. Neuro exam is grossly intact. Wounds healed. Splints in place. At this point she is still getting PPN through the NG, but her mucosa is ugly. She was on the schedule yesterday for a PEG but finally woke up. She is on Prevacid, Bactrim, propranolol, sub-Q heparin, and a little Ativan due to minor agitation when she came to yesterday. We've also got her on D5 half-normal saline at one hundred cc's per hour and twenty of potassium with that. I think—"

"Tiny, what is your assessment and plan?" Henry interrupted.

"Seeing as my priorities are always straight, the NG needs to come out and we need to get some chicken soup in her the old-fashioned way. Ortho should take the splints off—er, wait, her bones are probably brittle from disuse, so OT and PT should see her first. The Foley should also come out. In terms of meds and fluids, we should probably only keep the propranolol."

Declan tried to remain detached. "What do you think about the junky lungs?"

"Oh yeah, probably a little atelectasis, so we need to get her coughing. I doubt it's pneumonia with a normal temp. I guess she could be in failure, but that would be unusual for either her age or Dec's aortic repair. We'll watch it."

"I agree with Tiny," John said. "Dec?"

"Sounds good."

Rounds ended. On their way to La Estacion for breakfast, Declan told Tiny to make sure the girl was also seen by social services. "There is no reason she shouldn't be off our service early next week," he added.

As he poured everyone a cup of coffee, Henry said, "Dude, I miss the students. They were both pretty good, huh?"

"Yeah, 'We miss the students,'" John retorted as he simultaneously raised his eyebrows and cupped both sides of his chest, making reference to Abby's last-minute busty display. They all smiled. "I know I'm being an asshole and totally inappropriate, but shit, I had a boner all day yesterday. What is up with that?"

"I'll tell you what's up," Tiny said. "Two things: One, she is a babe of the sort that we won't see on this team or on any other one in the near future. Chicks that hot and that smart don't come by too often in this business. And two, after tonight, Declan is going to be letting us know whether Abby was wearing panties under her scrub pants the last couple of days. My money's on no."

"What?" Henry frowned at Dec.

"It's just dinner, man. Tiny, how the hell do you know?" Declan asked.

"Hey, man, my almost three hundred pounds of flesh are not a figment of your imagination. I am present, aware, happenin', and I always know who's doing who."

Dec shook his head and smiled. "Tiny, you are one big, freaky dude."

John tossed his napkin on the table and changed the subject. "Anyhow, I heard Brian and the trauma teams had some real fubars after the Texas City incident." Before John finished, they all whispered in unison: "Fucked up beyond all recognition." John waited until the laughter subsided and then continued. "Anyway, there were a lot of bad traumas that night. We all did a lot of good."

Tiny scowled. "Man, you are getting touchy-feely. Go away and be a family doc or something. Fuck! You are a goddamn surgeon. That's what we do. We fix people. What do you want? A kiss? A pat on the back?"

"Tiny, you suck. I was just having a moment," John said.

"Well, go have it far away from here—you know, where someone cares."

As usual, they continued to fling verbal garbage for a while, laughing all along, before they each went home to get some rest and do it all over again the next day.

NINE

// Hmm, I kind of pictured you as a pickup truck sort of guy," Abby said as Declan gentlemanly opened the passenger door of his 1983 canary-yellow Mercedes-Benz 240D.

"Well, I inherited this car. It's a long story."

She settled in the passenger seat and grinned at Dec. "Great! You have between now and your rounds tomorrow morning to tell it to me."

Dec closed her door and, as he walked around the front of the car, had a queasy moment. He was thinking about how he had been on only about a dozen dates since high school. But the moment dissipated once he turned on the ignition and started off toward the causeway. A corner of his mouth turned up a bit. Dec realized he was on a date with one of the most striking women on campus.

I got up to make us more tea, while Frank gave Rif a couple of treats.

"That's it, buddy, no more," Frank told the dog. "So, did Dec and Abby get it on?"

"Why am I not surprised you'd say that?" I shook my head at him, a mischievous smile on his face. But I continued with the story. "Declan told me their tentative plan was to have dinner at Pappas Seafood House, about thirty-five minutes from Galveston.

It happened to be in the same shopping center as the theater, so going to a movie would have made a nice ending to the evening. Interestingly, though, Abby kept talking about his car. As you will see, this caused them to miss all available showtimes."

"That sounds promising," Frank said, splashing a little lemon into his fresh cup of tea.

"That odometer can't be right," Abby said, peering at the dashboard. The odometer registered sixty-six thousand. "How old is this baby?"

"You won't believe it when I tell you that this car is twenty-two years old and that these"—he pointed to the odometer—"are kilometers."

"No way. That's like forty thousand miles. How is that possible?"

"The car belonged to my mother. It was an anniversary gift from my dad. This was a long time ago, in Mexico City. But a few years later, my dad passed away, and my mom and I moved to Houston, where one of my uncles helped us establish a business. My mom bought a van for the business, and for some reason, it became the only vehicle she ever used. Except for the occasional weekend trip, this car was parked most of the time. Then, for my birthday, sophomore year of high school, she gave me a card and a little box with the car keys inside. I basically only drove it for about a year because I ended up going to Yale for college. I didn't need a car there, so I left it at home. I came back to Texas for med school and residency here in Galveston. The car has still been parked most of that time too. As you have noticed the last month, I don't get out much."

"So, it's practically new," she exclaimed.

"Yeah, pretty much."

By this time, they had each ordered dinner. She opted for the blackened mahi-mahi on dirty rice, and he went for the fried seafood platter with french fries.

"The next bypass you perform may be on yourself," she pointed out.

"Hey, when on my deathbed, I want to look back and say, 'Yeah, it was short, but those fried clams were worth it.'" Dec was smiling.

"Anyway, that first day at La Estacion, I was a bit intrigued with your being born in Texas but growing up in Mexico. Now with that car thing, I really want to know more, especially about your parents. How did they meet?"

— ~~ —

Declan was initially hesitant and started off with superficial anecdotes. But Abby wanted to know more. So, eventually, he sat back and gave her a fairly detailed summary of his parents' story.

"In the early seventies, my father was a manager at Cementos de Mexico, a gigantic producer of cement and other concrete derivatives. The assignment that would make him vice president of his division temporarily sent him to San Francisco. At the time, there was a movement there to reinforce public structures in order to make them more earthquake resistant. So, he spent a considerable amount of time there, you know, wheeling and dealing.

"One day, his business counterpart invited him over for a barbecue. That man must have really liked my dad because, more than anything, that gathering was a setup. That guy's wife was hosting a close friend of hers who was visiting from Ireland. Well, that friend answered the door when my dad showed up. I remember my dad saying that his jaw dropped in disbelief when he saw her because he wasn't expecting his business counterpart, who was older than my dad, to have such a young and beautiful wife. Before my father had a chance to say anything, the host couple walked up behind the mystery woman. As soon as he saw them, he breathed an internal sigh of relief. The couple then greeted him and introduced my dad to the woman who would later become my mother."

Declan opened his wallet. "I carry a little picture of us. Here, check it out. Just don't laugh. I was about five or six—hey! I told you not to laugh!"

"I can't help it. You are adorable," Abby said.

"Ouch! Don't say that. I prefer *handsome.*"

"No, no, no. Your dad was handsome. And your mother? Wow. I'm truly speechless."

"Thank you," he said.

"But please, go on. I want to hear the rest of their story."

"Obviously, they hit it off," he said. "Almost every day for a couple of weeks, they ate out together, caught a show at the Orpheum, and rushed through several museums. Apparently, though, what really did it were the evening walks around Golden Gate Park. They were among dozens of other twosomes strolling serenely on those unfailingly beautiful San Francisco summer evenings. There, surrounded by faintly lit park lanterns, they held hands for the first time.

"The day my dad was supposed to return to Mexico, he called to request a week of vacation. The business deal had gone well, so his request was no problem. They rented a car and did the standard drive down the Pacific Coast Highway. On their way back from Santa Barbara, they were captivated by the sight of two whales whose spouts appeared in the distance, side by side. As sappy as that sounds, they took it as a sign and realized that they did not want to leave each other. They arrived in Carmel at sunset. They sat on the beach for hours, thinking about how things could work out."

"Sounds like they were pretty sure they were in it for good," Abby said. "To me, it sounds tough: Mexico, Ireland, a three-week relationship?"

"That's what I would've said too. Yet it wasn't tough at all. In fact, that night on the beach, my mom told my dad that her love for him was stronger than all the concrete his company could possibly produce. It's kind of corny, but after she said that, my dad immediately took off his university ring, went down on one knee, and grabbed her hand. The ring was too big for her ring finger, so instead, he placed it on her thumb. With a smile on her face and joy in her heart, she said yes. Serenaded by a flock of seagulls above them, they kissed.

"In a nutshell, they each flew home at the end of that week. Back in Mexico, my father had barely received his first love letter from overseas when he picked my mom and my Irish grandparents up from the airport three weeks later. Like me, my mom was an only child. My dad had two brothers who, as a relevant fact, happen to be doctors. Unlike most Mexican families, my father's was not particularly large. So, my parents had a small, elegant, uncomplicated, and obviously Catholic wedding in Cuernavaca—a beautiful city known for its eternal spring climate, just outside of Mexico City.

"It's funny. Apparently, my Irish grandparents loved Mexico so much that they found it hard to leave one month later. Not to mention the fact that they were leaving their only daughter behind. In a way, though, they were glad to see her get out of Ireland. The seventies were terrible there—the religious conflict in Northern Ireland was making a mess of everyday society, including basic safety. The UK was generally in economic chaos with skyrocketing inflation and unemployment. The fact that my mom had fallen in love with my dad and landed in a peaceful country was comforting to my grandparents. They visited us a few times after I was born, but they died before I was old enough to remember them."

"Wait. So how do you and Texas come into the picture?" Abby asked.

"Well, after all, my dad did get a promotion at work. This required him to travel quite a bit. They were able to do it together, and for a couple of years, they really enjoyed it. His job took them to practically every state in Mexico and several others here in the US and Canada. Anyway, somewhere between the Yukon and the Yucatán, I came to be. During a six-month stint in Laredo, Texas, I was born at the venerable Mercy Hospital. It was at that point when they decided that a nomadic lifestyle would probably screw me up. Soon after, we returned to Mexico City. My dad quit the company and took a job teaching economics at El Colegio de México, a prestigious university there. I grew up. We were all very happy."

"How did you end up living in Texas?"

"I'm getting there, hang on," Dec said. "One night, when I was ten, our family dog started scratching under my bedroom door. She usually slept on the bed with my parents, so I thought it was a bit strange. I got up to let her in, but as the door opened, she just stood there looking at me. Then I heard some voices coming from the living room downstairs. I went to the balcony and saw my uncle and aunt sitting beside my mother with their arms around her. They were all crying. I had never seen my mother that upset before. In fact, she only shed tears when she was too happy. In my gut, I knew something had happened to my father. So, I did what any ten-year-old would've done under the circumstances. I hugged the dog." Dec paused to take a breath. "My gut had been right. My dad died in a car accident that day."

"Oh my God. I'm so sorry." Abby instinctively reached out to touch Declan.

"It's okay. It was hard for me at first, but time does heal. When I think of my dad now, I smile. All the memories I have of him are great. It was more difficult for my mother, though. Although she once told me that she could go forever on their love and her own memories, she was never quite the same. This brings me back to what started the whole conversation—the low mileage on my car.

"As I said before, my dad had given her the car a year earlier as an anniversary present. That year we started taking short road trips to nearby parks. My mom would pack a picnic basket. My dad would pack books, the dog, and his kite—in case the wind was good. I would load up my bike and skates. When it was time to eat, we would all sit in a circle and my mom would pass out the goodies. The two of them always poured themselves a glass of wine and me a glass of Tang. Remember Tang? Anyway, before we all drank, she would invariably give the dog a treat and say something sappy like, 'You three are the loves of my life.' She would wink at my dad, point her finger in turn at the dog and me, and then continue, saying, 'Shame on you for making me steal all the happiness in this world.' This sounds more powerful in Spanish—which by then she had mastered as her own.

"The car was tied to so many happy memories for our family. But I think once my father was gone, those memories only reminded her of how much she'd lost. That's why I think my mom seldom used the car afterward."

—∿∿—

When Declan reached that point of his parents' story, they were on their way back to Galveston and tears had formed in Abby's eyes. After she wiped them away, Dec completed the story by telling her that, at the urging of one of his uncles, who had done a surgical residency at Baylor and settled in Houston, Declan, his mother, and their dog had moved to Texas for good.

As he turned into Abby's apartment complex, Dec was silently perplexed. *Shit!* he thought. What the hell possessed me to get so damn personal with Abby? And worse, why on earth am I thinking of Lauren?

They did not kiss on that first date.

TEN

Turning points are often the result of some sort of test.

In this case, quite literally, it was the in-service examination for surgical residents. This was a yearly national exam administered by the American Board of Surgery to gauge the progress of resident training. Every resident took the same exam, but scores were based on the level of training. For example, although first-year residents would take the same exam as fifth-years, their scores would be based only on the performance of all first-year residents across the country. In most surgery programs, the results did not become part of the doctor's file. These tests were simply used so that residents would identify and address their weaknesses. General surgery programs were usually five years. Therefore, residents underwent this all-day testing extravaganza a grueling five times.

For Declan's team members, unlike most surgery programs, the exam results became part of their permanent dossier. Having gone through the same headache himself, Dec usually gave his more senior residents two days off before the exam so they could gather their thoughts, study a bit, and transition to a paper-and-pencil frame of mind. In short, this meant Declan and Tiny had to run their entire service for those two days. Tiny could forgo the first two days because a potentially low score did not affect him as much. As an intern, a modest score on the exam was more prudent so he'd show improvement over the next four years. But he did have to take the exam on the third day. Dec would have to run clinic by himself on the day of the test.

Bottom line? These two days required meticulous, smart, and felonious inconspicuousness. Nobody outside the team could be aware of the residents' "time off." Giving his guys this break was an exception, not the rule; surgeons had to deal with any challenge before them, no matter how arduous, without missing a step. So, Declan rearranged surgeries, conferences, and rounds so that nobody, including Dr. Katz, would notice that Henry and John were MIA.

On his way to the wards, the first day without his residents, Declan ran into the neurology team in the elevator and, ostensibly, into a crossroads in his life. They gave him two fate-altering pieces of information.

One: Lauren was fully awake, coherent, and communicating. Two: she had a fever.

Declan arrived at the nurses' station. Out of habit, he greeted everyone around, including the janitor, and took Lauren's chart off the rotary rack. He turned to the last progress note, written by the medical student on the neurology team. It couldn't have been more complete. He reviewed all the data—from vital signs to her physical exam—but mulled over the last two components of the med student's note.

Assessment:
Prolonged hospital course with multiple surgical issues, now resolved. Normal neurological status. Of note are decreased breath sounds on the left and a fever of uncertain etiology.

Plan:
No need for further neurological consultation. Will sign off our service. Consider continued physical therapy given limb disuse. Fever workup. Surgical team aware.

"Hey, Dr. Bal, where's the gang?" the station secretary asked and snapped him out of his pensive state.

"Oh, they are all over the place. After the Texas City thing, we had to change things a little."

"I know. You guys must be sleeping even less now."

"We make do."

Despite the casual conversation, all he could think about was that with the guys presently out of the picture, he would have to talk to Lauren himself. Declan could no longer just hear about her status and distantly agree or disagree with her treatment plans. Furthermore, the fever would extend her stay in the hospital until its cause was found and resolved.

He knocked lightly on the door and entered her room. Sitting up on the bed, Lauren reflexively glanced at him. While completely motionless, she felt subconsciously startled—as if her body had jolted backward. Unlike her reaction to others who had recently come into the room, her first conscious look at Declan instantly and inexplicably froze her mind and body.

"Good morning. I am Dr. Baltierra. I'm one of the many doctors taking care of you. I understand you are feeling better lately," Declan said as he approached her bed. As was his custom, he found a spot on the edge of the bed and sat down briefly to discuss her condition. "Unfortunately, you have developed a fever, and we need to find out where it's coming from. We will be running some blood tests and taking some X-rays." He paused to allow her to process what he had said so far. "I suspect it is related to a touch of pneumonia, but I need to make sure that it is not related to your graft—you know, related to the surgery."

Declan got up slowly and began to examine her, starting with her surgical wounds. They looked mostly healed. He auscultated her abdomen and listened to her lungs. Indeed, she had decreased breath sounds at the base of her left lung. This was reassuring. Unlike a run-of-the-mill pneumonia, a surgical graft infection would be extremely difficult to treat without surgery.

"Any problems?" he asked.

"No," she answered in a soft, protracted tone.

"Well, either Tiny—I mean, Dr. Haley—or I will be by later this evening to see how you are doing." He gave Lauren the reassuring smile he gave all his patients on rounds, turned around, and went out the door.

—m—

Lauren sighed in regret. All she had managed to mutter was that simple "no."

She was confused and didn't know exactly how to react, for she knew that Declan was not just "one of the many doctors." He was the reason she was still alive. But she didn't know whether to say "Thanks" or "I'm sorry for all the trouble" or "What exactly did you operate on inside me?" or, for that matter, "Help!"

She closed her eyes and again began to recall the events that had brought her to the hospital. Her most immediate recollections involved getting picked up by folks she barely knew from her job at a thrift store. They offered her a lift and the promise of unrestrained fun in Galveston. She joined them without question and shared alcohol and a number of unknown pills. This was how she'd spent nearly every weekend for the past year. It all started when she and her best friend, Sandra, decided to leave the quiet town of Victoria, Texas, for the shining and cosmopolitan city of Houston.

Lauren had attended a few semesters at the local college in Victoria and hoped to continue her education in Houston. She'd been living with her brother and his unsympathetic and eternally confrontational wife. Their mother had passed away several years before. They never knew their father. Therefore, Lauren felt she had nothing to lose in venturing off to Houston.

The pair arrived via Greyhound. Two weeks later, with the help of want ads, they found a relatively inexpensive apartment in a borderline-safe neighborhood in the city's north end. Both found jobs as waitresses and began their new lives in their new environment. Lauren even registered for classes at Houston County Community College—where she would, ironically, begin a downward spiral.

She was still young, naïve, impressionable, and girdled by the stigma of small-town life. The desire to learn, think, explore, and find herself culminated in an association with a group of students who were big on social causes and self-expression. They had a bunch of noble-sounding ideas, but really, they were a dozen young people who were mad at life. Their backgrounds were irrelevant. The fact is that their meetings revolved around hate. They denounced racism, sexism, and exalted the poor—but had a violent loathing for those who they thought were to blame.

Lauren stuck with the group, hoping it would eventually extend beyond its chaotic finger-pointing. She had read about successful student movements that included food drives, seminars, recycling campaigns, and other constructive, inclusive agendas. But she was neither secure in her own ideas nor mature enough to realize that whatever she was looking for wasn't among these people. They spent their time talking about what they hated. Their money was spent on tattoos and body piercings, just because they thought tattoos and piercings alone would make them subversive. When that didn't satisfy them, they eventually moved on to drugs. Invariably, the drugs circulated through the whole organization. While initially reluctant, Lauren succumbed to the intense peer pressure and ultimately joined in.

After a few months, the group's effect on Lauren became hard for Sandy to ignore. Late one afternoon, Lauren dragged herself out of bed and into the kitchen for something to eat. She walked in to find Sandy sitting at the table with a grim, concerned look on her face.

"Honey, what the fuck are you doing? You look like shit. There is a message from work asking where you are. As far as

I know, you dropped the two classes you signed up for, and I'm afraid to ask you for this month's share of the rent."

"You sound like my sister-in-law. Everything is okay. I am just tired lately."

"There is tired, and then there is sleeping for two days straight. I hope that bunch of idiots you hang out with are not poisoning you or something."

They were poisoning not only her but themselves as well. Lauren didn't exactly know at what point the winds of fate—and her decisions—carried her away from everything that was good. Eventually, she lost her apartment, her job, her best friend, and her reason for being. She returned to her hometown of Victoria for a short time, but the lack of support and her new addictions drove her back to Houston. The college group that started it all had broken up by then. She was completely on her own.

Lauren skittered from odd job to odd job, from one grimy apartment or shelter to another. This period of her existence kept her on a roller coaster whose tracks circled around addiction. Her thoughts became gradually more difficult to sort out. She often found herself around people who were dangerous. This combination of factors, on a night that was supposed to be suffused with the unabashed jubilation of Mardi Gras, culminated in a ride on a Life Flight helicopter.

Now, with her eyes closed as she lay in a hospital bed, it was very easy for Lauren to see all the missteps and poor choices she had made over the past year. Choices that had almost ended her life. Suddenly, in the midst of all these thoughts swirling in her mind, she opened her eyes. In an electrifying convergence of feelings, Lauren realized that she did not crave drugs.

A month in a coma had wiped her system clean.

For a split second, the glass seemed half full. But then, the actual situation and thoughts of her uncertain future rushed in, sending her back into abysmal emptiness.

ELEVEN

Talking to a patient had never been so difficult.

From the moment Declan signed a short progress note in her chart, he went through the rest of the day as efficiently as an automaton. Lauren's heart had physically been in his hands, but the simple feel of his palm on her shoulder while listening to her lungs sent him into a kind of trance. Once again, he was faced with having to account for feelings that could not simply be pinned on pity. These were the same confusing feelings that, not too long ago, had prompted him to avoid emotional trouble and make every effort to discharge her from his service.

Had it not been for Tiny, who was able to see Lauren at evening rounds, that well-defined border between his mind and his heart would have faded even faster than it already was.

―――

That night Abby ordered for both of them. It had been three days since their dinner date.

"My friend here will have the General Tso's chicken, shrimp fried rice, and an egg roll. Oh, extra grease on everything, please." She winked at the kid behind the counter and smiled at Dec. "I will have the Moo Goo Gai Pan with steamed rice."

"Drinks?" the kid asked.

"Just water, thank you," Abby replied.

They had returned from one of their on-again evening runs and decided on General Joe's Chopstix, a fast-food place on the seawall with a balcony that overlooked the Gulf. They got their waters and went upstairs to find a seat. They continued a conversation about Abby's new rotation in pediatrics.

"Yeah, all I remember from pediatrics is being afraid of dropping a kid," Declan said. "Everything is so different. Doses are a pain in the ass. Not to mention trying to diagnose a kid who just cries and can't talk to you."

"But they are so cute. And I don't even like kids." Abby took a sip of water. "You know what's even harder? Dealing with the parents. You have to make them happy. The other day, we basically ended up giving a kid antibiotics for a viral infection—just because the mom insisted on having them."

"It's the same in the ER. People wait for hours to be seen, so for God's sake, let's give them an X-ray they don't need. Which, surprisingly, often does make them feel better." Declan smirked.

The food arrived.

"Yeah," Abby said, "until all the bacteria are so used to our antibiotics that everything we have stops working."

"Perfect," Declan joked. "Time to develop new and expensive antibiotics. The drug companies wouldn't have it any other way. *Capitalism*, I love it."

"How sarcastic of you, Dec. So, on to a different subject, what are the guys up to?"

"If I tell you, I will have to kill you."

"Oh, come on," Abby pleaded. "They are the coolest crew I've rotated with."

He told her about the exam and the whole under-the-table time-off situation.

"Dec, once again, for a surgeon, you are okay." She grinned.

Declan looked at her dazzling smile. In a flash, he also studied her appealing, straw-blond hair in a perfect ponytail. He observed her alluring facial features—starting with her lustrous and engaging green eyes. He contemplated her effortless sensuality, even in workout gear. Additionally, she was witty and smart—in and out of the practice of medicine. *Why am I not head over heels for this nice, smart, beautiful woman?* Declan thought. Without giving a hint of his silent pondering, he replied to her comment, "Gee, I suppose I should take that as a compliment."

"Of course. That's how I meant it."

— ᴍ —

The corner of Market and 4th was the point where they each split off and walked to their respective apartments. Lately, as they spent more time together and began to individually grapple with the meaning of their relationship, this corner had become slightly awkward. Just as they approached the parting point that night, Abby took the edge off by inviting Declan to a baseball game.

"As you know, my family is loaded, and we own a box at the ballpark. This Saturday the Astros play LA. What do you say?"

"I say I'm rooting for the Dodgers," Dec responded.

"What?"

"Well, when you are a kid in Mexico City, you grow up a Dodgers fan for baseball, a Cowboys or Raiders fan for football, and a Lakers fan for basketball. Don't ask me why—that's just the way it is. Somehow that has kind of stuck with me."

"Whatever floats your boat, man. Listen, I love your car and the stories behind it. But you drive painfully slow. I'll pick you up. Around five?"

"Okay," Declan replied.

Without another word, they parted.

Abby couldn't resist. She had only walked a quarter of a block before her feet turned her around. Despite her better intuition, she returned to the street corner, hoping Declan would still be there waiting. In a girlish rush, she wished for a romantic embrace—the sort that only seems to occur in the movies. But she stood there, watching as he walked ever so distantly away.

Declan did not take her for granted. It certainly wasn't a lack of attraction either. He really liked Abby, but he was out of step with his heart. The truth is, he had never actually been in love. His previous relationships had never shown him what it really was, when it happened, or what to do about it. With Abby's eyes still boring into his back, he was addressing this very issue in his mind. He told himself that whatever Lauren—*I mean, Abby*— meant to him, must be given a chance.

He turned the corner without looking back.

TWELVE

On the second day without John and Henry, Tiny was over-whelmed with the floor patients. After rounding on the ICU, Declan's next stop was Lauren. He picked up the chart and reviewed the latest information. She still had a fever, and the radiology report showed that she had a pleural effusion—fluid between her lung and chest cavity—not pneumonia.

Shit! he thought. *What now?* He went to the radiology monitor to check the images himself. Sure enough, the X-rays showed fluid layering along her side and her otherwise clear lungs. At this point he had to start entertaining the possibility of a graft infection. He ordered a urine test and a CT scan and asked a nurse to start empiric antibiotics. In addition, he had to analyze the fluid in her chest to exclude the possibility that this was infected. He got a procedure consent form and headed toward the room. As before, he knocked at the door—but despite the lack of an answer, he entered anyway.

Lauren was not on the bed. The bathroom door was cracked. As he approached and peered inside, Declan realized that after all this time, he'd forgotten a very important thing—a psychiatry consult. She was on the floor, naked. Her gown was bunched up beside her. Lauren was crying softly and holding with one hand the thin fiberglass strip that had covered the surgical scar on her chest. This extended from just below her collarbone to just above her abdomen. The fiberglass was a treatment mainly used to keep scars on burn victims as smooth as possible, but Declan had customized this simple device for her.

Until now, she had been bathed at the bedside. She had done well with the latest physical therapy, so she had gotten the okay from her nurse to take a shower by herself that morning. Nobody gave a second thought to the fact that Lauren was a twenty-four-year-old woman with a new, long surgical scar in the middle of her chest. Even though Declan made every effort to make the wound as cosmetically acceptable as possible, she was still ill-prepared for her first glance in the mirror. It was hard to miss the angry-red, lumpy scar. Like welded metal, it was etched starkly up and down her chest.

As on her first conscious encounter with Declan the previous day, she was again taken aback when she saw him enter and kneel beside her. After a quick glimpse at his compassionate eyes and attentive demeanor, she had to look away. She couldn't face him.

Declan picked up her gown and put it back on her. Then he lifted her in his arms and brought her out to the bed. He sat on the stool next to her, one hand on her shoulder and the other between her hands.

During this brief silence, she felt mortified—not at having been naked in front of him, but rather at her sudden inability to cope with her situation. Her initial consternation about the healing wound on her chest suddenly turned to embarrassment, as she did not want to burden Declan with yet another one of her problems. He just looked at her, concerned, wishing he had considered this earlier. Watching her gather herself, trying to rein in her tears, he scrambled for the right thing to say.

Declan began quietly. "I'm awfully sorry, but it was the only way we—"

"I know. I just…I will be fine."

"It may not seem so now, but with time and some treatment, it will eventually look much, much better."

"Yes. I know. I'm sorry," she said. There was silence again, and then Lauren said in a near whisper, "I deserve this."

This was not the first time Declan had to deal with postsurgical emotional scars. Unlike most surgeons whose attitudes were to do a good technical job and to leave the crying for someone else's shoulder, he felt his patients' pain in his own heart. His empathy invariably soothed most of his patients. With Lauren, however, he was overwhelmed. From the moment she said those last words, he knew this was a job for a professional counselor. She was still a lost soul in need of drug rehab. And on top of that, she currently had a disfiguring scar.

Task at hand: focus and change the subject, Declan thought.

"Things are difficult for you right now," he said, "but my primary concern is to make sure you are physically well. You don't seem to have pneumonia. Basically, there is some fluid in your lungs, which we need to make sure is not infected. So, I need to get a sample of it to send to the lab for analysis."

Lauren's eyes were lowered, looking at her hands, and only occasionally did she raise them to look at Declan. When she did, it allowed him to get a good look at her face. He recalled her appearance the night she had first arrived. Now, all her metallic piercings had been removed. Her hair had grown out to show its natural black color that, in turn, framed a pair of vivid brown eyes. The faintly shifting sunlight through the window created undulating shadows on her face and skin. They reminded Declan of sand dunes in a desert—desolate and beautiful.

He refocused and continued, "The way I do this is by numbing the skin on your back over the bottom part of the left lung. It's an injection of lidocaine. Then I introduce a needle and a small catheter that will allow me to get a sample of the fluid." He reached for a clipboard with the consent form. "I do need your permission to do this, as there are a few risks you need to be aware of…"

He covered the risks in detail. She nodded and reached for the pen.

"Do you have any questions?"

"No," Lauren said and then signed the form.

"Hang in there. I will step outside to get things ready."

"May I shower first?" she asked.

Declan turned to her from the door, pondering the previous scene and answered, "Sure, go ahead."

This gave him time to see other patients and catch up with Tiny. He also asked an aide to page Dr. Jacques.

———m———

Dec and Tiny were sitting in a small conference room going over patient data.

"So, you bangin' her yet?" Tiny probed.

Dec was caught off guard. Then he realized Tiny was referring to Abby. "None of your business, stud."

"Hey, man, we at least need an answer on the underwear thing. I got money riding on that!"

"Dude, we've got a service to run here. Get out of the gutter."

"All right, all right. Look, I'll trade you Ms. Madison's thoracentesis for Mr. Stein's central line."

Declan thought about that for a second. "No, I got this one. Besides, you need to start getting comfortable putting in lines. Have you done one before?"

"I've seen a couple," Tiny answered.

"There you go, 'See one, do one, teach one.' You are all set."

"Fuck it. You are right. I'm up for that, captain. I'll make you proud." The telephone on the table rang and Tiny answered. "Hey, Dec, did you page a Dr. Jacques?"

"Yeah, thanks," Dec said and took the phone. He exchanged pleasantries with the person on the other end and then got right to the point. "Listen, I have a favor to ask you. I know we need to request consults through the psych service, but I dropped the ball a little bit and I need to make amends, fast. There is a young woman on my service who was sort of stuck in purgatory. You know, drugs and stuff. After passing through my operating room and a median sternotomy later, she has definitely fallen a little closer to hell. She's got issues that I can't cut out with a scalpel. I'm wondering if you could give me a hand with this one." He quickly glanced at the front of the chart before him. "Room 624. Her name is Lauren Madison. By the way, how are the kids?" There was a short pause. "Good, I'm glad." Pause. "Oh, my mom is fine, you know, her usual routine with the business." Pause. "My regards and a hug for Julie. Thanks again."

"Who was that?" Tiny asked.

"Sam Jacques, the chief of adolescent psychiatry. We were in the same med school class."

"Oh yeah, that smart dude. The one who published so many papers during residency that they made him associate professor and division chief right off the bat? I bet he is making a lot more cash than you are, bro."

"Well, if he is not, his wife definitely is. Julie is a psychiatrist in private practice near Clear Lake. Met in school, and now they have kids and a dog and a minivan…"

"Scary!"

"Yeah, I guess," Declan said.

"'I guess'? Dec, don't go flimsy on me. Dogs and minivans, being whipped, fuck, I'd rather poke my eye with a toothpick. You are still my hero—love 'em and leave 'em, dude. The Fonz meets Humphrey Bogart. Living large. Please, don't go soft on me, or else." Tiny raised his hand to his head and curled his index finger as if pulling a trigger.

"You are freakin' crazy, you know that?" Declan said with a self-conscious smile.

Tiny rubbed his chin. "Wait a minute, that's not it. Is it? Spill baby, spill. Give it to me."

"What?" Declan asked innocently.

"Do I look stupid to you?"

"Okay, so I dated Sam's wife, Julie," Dec conceded.

"Do I have a knack for shit like this or what?" Tiny prodded some more. "So…?"

"So nothing." Declan flipped a page on the chart then looked thoughtful. "I guess she realized that I was going to be a surgeon and have the lifestyle of the sort you are starting to get used to by now."

Tiny beamed. "Hell, I love my fucked-up life. I get to cut people and eat junk all day. All on very few hours of sleep. It's like a dream come true!"

"Precisely because of dreams like that, she dumped me."

"Someone dumped your ass? Wow. It's like Miss Moneypenny turning things around on James Bond." Tiny shook his head, pretending to look stunned and in disbelief.

—⋘—

The matter had been simple. It hadn't been the prospect of a surgeon's lifestyle. Julie had been in love with Declan. They'd been together most of their third year—a demanding period of medical school—when students must not only begin the hands-on task of taking care of patients but also master the basic theory behind each medical specialty. Most students made it—albeit with a wide array of wounds. Those who could withstand the deepest gashes went into surgery. The ones who could tolerate only superficial cuts went into internal medicine or related primary care fields. Those with painful reactions to minor scrapes opted for cushier fields like dermatology or ophthalmology. The smart ones, of course, avoided wounds altogether and went into radiology.

Fourth year was the light at the end of the tunnel. During this year, most rotations were taken on a pass/fail basis, and paradoxically, students assumed less responsibility than during the previous year. They became comfortable taking care of patients and enjoyed seniority around campus. It was basically a cruise year—a reward for surviving third year. Of course, depending on a student's chosen specialty, the fourth-year respite ended quickly at the start of a whole new level of punishment: internship.

In Declan and Julie's case, the first two months of their fourth year were a turning point. During that period, they actually had time to enjoy a wonderful relationship. They met each other's families. They had fun and supported each other in every way possible. They accepted each other's ideas and quirks. Sex was always new, exciting, and satisfying. They cared for each other deeply. One night, she said she loved him, and he responded with the four magic words. Yet there was something off about it. As soon as he said it, an inexplicable feeling washed over her—the kind of peculiar intuition that surpasses the meaning of spoken words.

Julie realized in that moment that, despite it all, he was not in love with her.

He would have married her if she'd asked. He would have done anything, at any cost to himself, to give her happiness. But she could not knowingly allow him to do that. Accepting that he did not actually love her as she loved him, Julie amicably broke off their relationship. She found the magic she deserved with Declan's good friend Sam.

—∿∿—

Lauren sat on the bed facing away from Declan and held on to her nurse, who stood in front of her. He cleaned the area with surgical antiseptic, covered her skin in the usual sterile fashion, and injected the anesthetic. Then he expertly introduced a Yueh catheter between her seventh and eighth left posterior rib space. *Damn*, he thought as he withdrew clear, obviously uninfected fluid. His last hope was for a clean CT scan and "dirty" urine. He did not want to have to operate on her again.

—m—

He worked the easiest thirty-six hours yet.

On the morning of the in-service exam, Declan was saved by the bell, or more specifically, by his pager. Dr. Katz wanted to inform him that a heart was landing as they spoke and that given the scarcity of surgical residents, he would be grateful for Declan's assistance. This meant that the outpatient clinic would have to be canceled. No music could be sweeter to his ears.

The transplant ended around five. He rounded on the usual patients and was pleasantly surprised when he read Lauren's negative CT scan and positive urine test. She had a simple urinary tract infection. The fluid in her lungs had been a red herring and insignificant. He felt comfortable leaving the fluid business alone, as in 20 percent of cases, no reason for the fluid accumulation is found. It would eventually go away on its own.

Surgeons live for the opportunity to operate. Cutting makes them tick. In fact, they love operating so much they see the clinic grind as just another way to shop for cases. With respect to Lauren, however, Declan felt awash with relief—he did not have to operate again. This time he allowed himself to feel a singular sensation of warmth and delight in knowing that she was getting better. He prescribed different antibiotics, did his best to suppress the emotions that surfaced in him whenever Lauren entered his mind, and called it a day.

The next day was Friday, an OR day. The troops were back, and Saturday could not come fast enough. John did the transport honors to and from breakfast. On the way back, Tiny was the first to be dropped off. Not surprisingly, as he made his way from the back seat of the two-door Honda Civic, he turned to Declan and declared with a cynical smile on his face, "Remember, dude. I am still counting on that information about Abby."

Tiny and Henry exchanged a spirited high five.

THIRTEEN

They had a twelve-person box to themselves. Abby procured wine, a platter of fresh fruit, and finger-sized quesadillas. The view along home plate and first base was extraordinary. If you looked immediately down from the box, you could see, besides the action around the diamond, what a night at the ballpark was really like. Children, clad in their team colors, waved banners emblazoned with the names of their favorite sluggers. Others sported fluorescent tubes around their necks, balloon hats, and the unforgiving traces of hot dog condiments all over their clothes. The much older "children" alternated between screaming at ungodly decibels about an umpire's judgment and gulping down industrial-sized cups of beer. There were horns and whistles and the sounds of radio broadcasts tuned to the game, at the game. Groups of college-aged men and women, intoxicated by either alcohol or team spirit, periodically appeared on the giant screen high above center field. You could hear praises and damnations when the stars on the field performed well or struck out. It was a tremendous show of energy and a chance to escape from the world, aided by the temporary protection of the massive retractable roof.

The Dodgers were losing.

Despite the score, Declan temporarily forgot the not-so-green turf of daily life outside the stadium. Interestingly, he did not feel like he was getting away from the daily responsibilities of operating or clinic or teaching or being taught or saving patients—he never saw his job as a nine-to-five grind. Every day and every patient and every relationship always brought something new. He loved that aspect of his job. Since his first day of classes as a brand-new medical student, and now, over ten years later, he thrived on getting up every morning no matter what day or how early. Some doctors thrive on the surgical profession. Declan was definitely one of those doctors. What, then, was the murky turf he was trying, albeit unknowingly, to escape from at the game?

There was only one distinct answer: Lauren.

From the moment circumstances essentially forced Declan to personally address her, he felt a compulsion to help. But how much more help did she need? He had extended Lauren's practically expired lease on life. The rest of her medical issues were being taken care of—even counseling, thanks to one of the best doctors in the field. How much more aid could he provide? How many more amends could he make or help her make? It would be unrealistic to think he could possibly repair whatever it was in her life that needed fixing.

Or worse, what if there was nothing to fix? Some people just made a short but satisfying life out of addiction. Declan had seen many cases beyond his help. In fact, much of his patient population shared a dependency on alcohol and tobacco. In these cases, he took care of their surgical issues with compassion and to the best of his technical ability. Beyond that, he simply called social services or made the appropriate referrals. Yet with Lauren, he felt a vague, slightly disturbing need to personally intervene. What was it about her that created this windmill of emotions? Perhaps, as it had occurred to him on innumerable occasions of late, it was not simply about helping her.

This internal conflict was why he needed to be at that game. This was why he uncorked a second bottle of wine. This was why it didn't matter that LA couldn't possibly come back from a 7–1 hole. This was why he did not mind it when Abby forced him up from his chair at the seventh-inning stretch and did not let go of his hand for the rest of the game.

That's baseball—a conglomeration of aversions, nonconformities, neglects, woes, misadventures, and in Declan's case, uncertainties that could be put on hold for nine gleeful and sporadically thrilling innings.

After the game, Abby did not want to end the night. Declan went along. Out of the parking lot, she turned right, and they made their way to the clubs on Southside Place.

Dance versions of hits from Everything but the Girl, Toni Braxton, and even Ricky Martin were in, and inhibitions were out. Abby was sexy yet glamorous, seductive yet charming. Dec was the envy of men and women alike. They got hooked on the lights and the tunes. There was a sharing of sweat and a few drinks in between. Contact turned into friction, and the rhythm turned brisk. They got lost in the moment.

In due course, all fun things must come to an end—in Texas, it happens at one a.m. The DJ announced last call. While music would play for an additional hour, it was time to go. At that point, Abby, Declan, and most of the other clubgoers realized that they were not particularly smashed. But they also knew that any sensible cop would surely slap them with a DUI if stopped.

Dec and Abby walked out and decided to sit on a bench in the brick-lined courtyard at the center of the ring of clubs. Music still reverberated over the horns and the screeching tires of the less prudent clubgoers, who were already getting behind the wheel. Other folks also chose a bench to regroup and decide on how best to get home, or how best to prolong the night's momentum.

"The last time I went out like this was as a med student," Declan said.

"Do you mean the last time you had fun, the last time you went out with someone, or the last time you were at a club?"

"All three," he replied.

"Is that good or bad?" Abby asked.

"I don't know."

She bumped her elbow against his side. "What are you talking about?"

"You know, with rounds and everything tomorrow…," he started to say.

"Which is still so far away. And we are so inebriated," she added with a smile.

Declan smiled back, in sad affirmation. "How long do you figure it would take to sober up?"

"Well, Doctor, as you should know, to completely sober up, until noon tomorrow. To safely pass a breath test and legally practice medicine, about three hours after drinking lots of fluids."

"Hmm. Four a.m. That puts us in Galveston by about five. Hey, it's not so bad. The boys are back, and I can show up around eight. I can even sleep a cushy three hours or so." Declan slid down on the bench as if it were a couch. He looked up, closed his eyes, and pretended to be asleep.

Abby stared at him. In that instant, she again beheld the understated and slightly exotic ruggedness of his face. The shimmer of the drying sweat on his wavy hair. His refined masculinity. She could not help but smile at his shoes. Not that anything was wrong with them—they were Italian, fit perfectly, and matched his outfit. This was just the first time she had seen him wear anything besides sneakers. Most of all, she thought about his brilliance, his character, his worthiness, his decency, his civility, and his and her own hearts. She pondered all this in the blink of an eye.

Abby reached into her purse. The rustling caused Dec to turn his head toward her and open one eye.

"What's up, Ab?"

She grabbed her phone, held it up with one hand, and pointed her opposite index finger at it. She softly bit her lip and looked at Declan's single open eye with an inquiring face.

"What? Looks like a phone."

"Dec, we can call a cab," she said.

"Oh no. I know you are rich and all, but just the principle of paying hundreds of bucks to get home? I couldn't do that. In fact, I'll probably be good to go pretty soon."

"Dec?"

"Really, I—"

"Dec, I want to call a cab, have you call Henry to tell him you will not be rounding tomorrow morning, get a hotel room, and spend the night with you."

The mostly silent ride to the nearby Westin Galleria had a hint of awkwardness. Nevertheless, her effort to hold his hand was met with a mutual sense of liberation and excitement.

—⁓m⁓—

A couple of hours passed.

"I feel like I should be lighting a cigarette right about now."

"Dec, I didn't know you smoked."

"I don't. But isn't that what cool people do in the movies after—you know?"

Abby had gotten up from the bed to join him on the balcony, which overlooked one of Houston's most fashionable enclaves. The downtown skyline was visible in the distance—with neon outlines on skyscrapers, it was a testament to Houston's wealth and excess. The rest of the city also seemed to glitter, as if it were an expanse of still ocean reflecting the stars of a vast and clear sky. A light wind from the nearby Gulf brought a refreshing break in the humidity. A steady flow of cars from the highway and the unfailing sound of sirens were Declan's only inkling of reality.

Abby wrapped her naked body around him as he leaned over the balcony's railing. Feeling the touch of her cheek on his bare back, he continued to stare out at the rapturous night—a night from which they did not emerge until very, very late the following afternoon.

At her request, perhaps knowing that it would prolong the trip, he drove. Their ride to Galveston was as silent as the taxi ride to the hotel. Abby's feelings were certain. She had fallen in love with him.

Declan stopped her car in front of Casa Caribe, the apartment complex where he lived. They exchanged sincere but conspiratorial smiles, and then both got out of the car. Declan stood by the driver's side as Abby made her way around the front of the car. He held the door open and grasped her hand to help her into the driver's seat, then gently closed the door and leaned through the open window. He caressed her impeccable golden hair. Then he met her lips for an absorbing yet revealing long time.

Just before he entered the apartment complex's gate, he turned around and waved goodbye. In return, she threw him an honest kiss into the wind.

—⁂—

Abby sped off, only to stop one block away on the last stretch of street facing the ocean. The radio was playing Bonnie Raitt's "I Can't Make You Love Me." She set her forehead against the steering wheel and silently broke into tears.

What had taken Julie Jacques more than a year with Declan to figure out, Abby realized in that one prolonged and revealing kiss. In spite of their agreeable runs by the shore, their always-congenial conversation, and an undeniably marvelous night, his caring reciprocity was only at the outskirts of true love.

As only fate and harsh reality were to blame, over the ensuing week, she found a way to sensibly yet painfully end their relationship.

FOURTEEN

Distraction can mean death in the surgical profession, so Declan kept himself in check during that emotionally tumultuous week. He felt confused and guilty when he realized that Abby was distancing herself. He never asked for an explanation. Because it would bring nothing but more pain, she never offered one either.

Declan was back to his introspective array of questions regarding Lauren. The signs of chronic disease were disappearing. People involved in her care commented on her new appearance. Some said that she was "actually quite pretty." Others said that she "now looks alive." Her nurses were glad to see that the "crappy hospital food" was "putting some flesh on those petite bones." Most folks, however, simply agreed that she looked "surprisingly clean, for a change." Of the many observations made about Lauren, what came to Declan's mind was a vague scent of—he thought for a second—fresh hibiscus.

Hibiscus, that palm-sized flower that grew on what seemed like a cross between tall bushes and short, branchy trees. It came in many colors and was often a symbol of brightness, tranquility, and joy. Except for one, most varieties had no distinct fragrance.

For Declan, the "scent" of hibiscus was his way to categorize what his senses experienced lately when he entered Lauren's room. It was more apparent when he had to come in brief contact with her—when he listened to her heart, when he looked at her eyes, when he felt her pulse in her neck, her wrists, her legs, and her feet. These few minutes transported him back to a time in his childhood when he would spend countless hours on a tiled patio, staring into a canopy of these singular and picturesque flowers. His mother loved hibiscus, especially the one variety known for its large blooms and fragrance. Every corner of the Baltierra patio and garden was colored with this kind of hibiscus. That patio was his retreat—like a sanctuary. Once there, he would close his eyes and inhale deeply, slowly. A near hypnotizing sensation would envelop him, and soon he would feel free. Happy. Loved—no matter the circumstance. Not surprisingly, Declan equated hibiscus to everything that was good.

Why these childhood recollections now? What was the connection? How did his feelings get tangled up in these intricate metaphors? Maybe the scent of hibiscus was not about his feelings but about those he subconsciously wished Lauren could experience. Now. Soon. Someday—for her sake.

Declan had continued to personally address Lauren's medical care. He told the team they did not have to make rounds on her. While this was one less patient for them to worry about, they could not help but wonder why. This added more weight to the burden on his shoulders, for he knew the team would soon want an explanation. An explanation, of course, that he did not have.

In the meantime, he knew everything about her health and her world within the hospital. He was afraid her life outside that sterile bubble would be dark and disappointing. Yet his conversations with her were mostly one-sided; Lauren was still reserved in her expressions, and she offered only a handful of words during their interactions. Most of these were simple yes and no answers. Perhaps she was hesitant about or did not know how to express herself regarding her current situation and, more importantly, her future.

Her days began at approximately six in the morning, when the first set of vital signs was taken. About an hour later, Declan would come in and perform his routine exam. These several minutes were difficult for her. She did not know why, after all this time, the person who had saved her life was taking hands-on care of her. It was difficult to know how to act in front of him. Lauren felt more at ease with the other members of the team. Dec always made her apprehensive, insecure, and even embarrassed. These were not strange feelings to her, but somehow they were accentuated in his presence. Then he would leave, and she would relax. Breakfast followed shortly after, and then she would take a shower.

From ten to noon, an orderly wheelchaired her to addiction meetings held in the behavioral sciences building. She traveled outside the John Sealy Towers, along the sidewalk, toward the Marvin Graves Building. This street was closed to car traffic. It was lined with beautifully manicured and colorful lawns and tall, leafy palm trees. The sun always shone splendidly on that short stretch, giving her a brief moment of happiness. Lauren had not seen the light of day—literally and metaphorically—for a long time. For the moment, this was all she had—her life and one peaceful city block. She would eat lunch with the rest of her therapy group. For thirty minutes to an hour after that, Lauren would disclose hard truths and hopeless sentiments to Sam Jacques in one-on-one sessions.

There was nothing truly extraordinary about Lauren's addiction. She had simply been with the wrong crowd at the wrong time in her life. Addiction was an inevitable side effect in a society where drugs were available and affordable. The way out of it was theoretically simple yet sometimes impossible: rigorous adherence and willingness to continue participating in meetings and support groups—in Lauren's case, even if her cravings seemed gone after being in a coma. Sam reiterated this fact. He did not have much to add on that subject. She would have to conjure up the willpower to resist future cravings, and to rely on others like her, who were in the process of winning battles against their own addictions.

What Sam also focused on was exploring the implications of her chest scar and its possible effects on her self-image. This had the potential to trigger a depressive state and thus start a vicious cycle that could eventually lead back to drugs. There was no single pill that could make the scar disappear. The regret associated with its cause had to be released.

This was why people like Sam Jacques existed. They were a wall, a sounding board. His job was essentially to listen—openly, liberally, and patiently.

The first session was short. Lauren did not have much to say right away. She opened up more in the second session. She was able to discuss her family, friends, surroundings, hopes, actions, and eventual pitfalls. Her past and present were utterly dysfunctional. This wasn't surprising. Her answers to Sam's open-ended questions didn't reveal any complicating factors such as physical, sexual, or emotional abuse. Therefore, this left him with the difficult task of exploring corners of her mind that could possibly harbor thoughts of suicide. This was the one thing no psychiatrist could miss. It was the one diagnosis that, when made correctly, could truly spare a life. Other physicians experienced this feeling every time they resuscitated a patient, whether in the emergency room, the operating theater, an intensive care unit, or the regular inpatient wards. It gave doctors a feeling of achievement and satisfaction, and was the justification for all the trials and tribulations that came with the profession.

Sam knew that Lauren had nothing to lose. He needed to make sure that her low self-esteem did not deteriorate into an inescapable pit, deepened by the scar she would see in the mirror for the rest of her life.

During one breakthrough session, Lauren eventually opened up. "Dr. Jacques. I'm grateful you are giving me the opportunity to talk about my life and my problems. I also know there is no simple answer to explain or excuse all that I have done. There also isn't a simple answer from you to help me get over things, change my ways, turn me around, and suddenly make me feel better."

"You are quite right, Lauren."

"I also know that you are here listening to me because Dr. Baltierra was worried about what this"—she placed her hand on her chest—"would do to my mind. Since I started seeing you, all the wonderful people taking care of me look at me like I am going to hurt myself. In fact, I get the feeling they have been specifically instructed to watch me closely for that reason."

Sam was candid. "You are, again, correct. I haven't quite placed you on suicide precautions, but I have asked that your medical team make an extra effort to track your emotions. You must understand that the facts surrounding your life and most immediate present merit this sort of concern. As you said, we are all trying to help you in the way that each of us has been trained to do so."

"I understand. And I appreciate it more than anything. But suicide is really far from my mind. I wish I had not done many of the things that put me here. My choices have left me in bad shape. On top of that, they've given me a permanent reminder of all that is wrong and dirty. But thanks to Dr. Baltierra, his team, and whatever higher power, if there is one, I'm still here. It's a sign that I'm not lost. I just have to find my way and my purpose. I can assure you that I don't want to go back to rock bottom again. It's too dark and cold and lonely." Lauren paused, sighed, and then continued. "Ironically, I am disappointed to be getting better every day. This means that soon there will be no reason for me to be here. I've never felt taken care of before. People here seem genuinely concerned for me. Everyone, from the people who clean up my room to Dr. Baltierra—they all make me feel like I am worth something. Worth living, at the very least."

Lauren stopped to think about what she had just said. She glanced up at Dr. Jacques.

"You may find it hard to believe, but I used to be a good, sensible person. I really want that again," she said. "Maybe I won't be satisfied with a small-town life, but I want to start from scratch. I don't know how, but at least I have a better idea of what not to do. When the lights go off at night and I hear the beeping of monitors and machines at the nurses' station across from my room, I tell myself that if everything else fails, I will never end up in some forsaken back alley with a dirty needle in my arm. So, don't worry about me that way. I know it's your job. But please believe that I will follow the right steps, remember all of you, and find myself again."

When she finished speaking, Lauren lowered her head and shifted her gaze toward her hands on her lap. This was the most she had ever spoken in therapy without being prompted. It may have also been her longest and most introspective assessment of her life. On the other hand, she had never had the opportunity to simply lie on a bed for weeks at a time, surrounded by four silent walls, and arrange her thoughts and emotions.

Opening up was not only a relief to Lauren but also revealing to Sam. It showed him that underneath the appearance of a twisted, thorny, and insecure self-concept, Lauren was quite centered. At the very least, she understood her mistakes. Furthermore, his gut feeling and clinical judgment told him that she was not a suicide risk, and the chest scar business would no longer be an issue.

That was one of her last sessions with Sam.

— ɯ —

As Lauren predicted, she would soon leave the hospital. This was the most distracting thought in Declan's mind that week. There was no reason for her to stay past the weekend.

After sharing her burdens in Sam's office, she was more articulate and conversant, and actually greeted Dec and inquired about the team. When he saw her during rounds on Friday, she had not only said thank you for the first time but also qualified it with sincere apologies "for the trouble and hard work—physical and intellectual" that she'd caused them. And she thanked Declan especially for appearing to love his job so much.

Something inside him wanted to explore what lay behind the curtain, behind the pierced and painted mask that had shown up in his operating room about a month and a half ago. That ethereal affinity toward her that night was haunting him again.

Still, first and foremost, he had to be professional.

On Saturday, rounds ended with Tiny's assessment and plan regarding Lauren's medical care.

"She can go on Monday," Tiny said.

"Dec?" Henry asked.

"I agree."

FIFTEEN

Declan and his mother had plans for dinner that Sunday. He left his apartment just before noon. He'd gotten a number of uptight notices and voicemails on his phone from the medical library, so he figured it would be a good time to stop by, return overdue books, and pay his fines before heading off the island. He parked in the circular driveway in front of the memorial garden. The garden was cradled between the library, a tall research building, the old classroom building, and the pharmacology department. Roses of all sizes and colors and in different stages of bloom were represented there. Small brass plaques on the ground identified each type. Declan's favorite was a hybrid tea rose known as the Olympiad, the traditional red rose.

—*m*—

"Flowers, you see, were, and probably still are, a very special and dear part of Declan's life," I told Frank.

"How so?" he asked.

"Well, I'm getting to that. But let's continue over dinner. I'm hungry."

I fixed us a couple of ham and swiss sandwiches, scooped out some leftover potato salad, and continued.

—*m*—

Declan's mother had made a fairly affluent living from their wholesale and retail flower business in Houston. Declan was not only familiar with the business but also held a great respect and love for roses. It's the flower that makes or breaks a florist. Roses had put him through college. When he started medical school, he would pass by the garden, read the plaques, and reminisce about working at the shop. In particular, he would remember those crazy days in February.

The week leading to Valentine's Day was always stressful. They had to coordinate the import, storage, and distribution of over thirty thousand roses. These came mainly from Colombia, Mexico, and California. They employed nine people and owned four vans. It was Declan's job to work out the logistics. Shipments would come to the two Houston airports. He had to coordinate every step between the arriving merchandise and customers' shops. There were always bad shipments, order errors, or refrigeration issues. When all the orders from the flower shops were filled, they switched gears and turned their attention to their own retail shop. They usually had about a hundred orders to fulfill. These would have to be arranged, stored, and delivered in a period of forty-eight hours before five p.m. on the fourteenth. Otherwise, the flower arrangements lost their fresh look and gave the shop a bad reputation. During high school, even if the two days before Valentine's were school days, he would take off to work the business. In college, he would fly home for a whole week to help out. After he started medical school, he no longer had that luxury. Declan was limited to making a quick call and offering moral support. But his mother made do.

At any rate, on those early February days before starting his medical career, Declan spent countless hours in front of a computer working out business details. Just before the big day, he joined the other folks in making and delivering flower arrangements. He loved seeing the faces of people receiving flowers. Whether the flowers were an expression of love or apology, people always seemed happy at that very moment. In the end, the Valentine's Day business accounted for half of his mother's yearly income.

Despite Declan's special connection to flowers, the library's rose garden no longer had the same effect on his memories. He had passed by it almost every day for nearly ten years.

During the early days of medical school, he made a point to go, see, and often study in it. Now, he only rushed through it and often went around it. That day, without giving it a second thought, he walked around the garden to get to the library. He went to the third floor and waited at the circulation desk.

"May I help you?"

"Yeah. I have a few books and this CD to return," Declan answered.

"You can just leave them at the counter."

"Well, I think I owe some money."

"Oh, in that case, let me check them in. God forbid I forgo the opportunity to make the library a few bucks. You know how that is." The young man at the counter smiled, rolled his eyes, and tilted his head at the librarian's office behind him. Mary Sanchez was an old-fashioned librarian who had been at UTMB for over thirty years and who considered it a sin to turn in overdue material without paying the fine. The young man proceeded to scan Dec's books. The computer beeped.

The clerk could not help himself. "Holy shit! Two months late. That comes out to, let's see, one hundred twenty-three dollars and thirty cents."

"Man, that sucks. Can I pay with a card?" Declan asked.

"Yeah, sure. Sorry, dude."

Just before Declan offered his card, a low and authoritative voice from behind a bookshelf said, "Wait a minute!" It was Dr. Katz, who emerged and made his way to the desk. "How do you do, Dec?"

"Just fine, Dr. Katz, thank you. Just taking care of a little debt problem. I wouldn't want library enforcement officers taking a bat to my kneecaps anytime soon."

"I overheard your predicament," Dr. Katz said. Then he addressed the fellow at the desk. "How do you do, son?"

"Fine, sir."

"Good. What I want you to do is to charge Dr. Baltierra's outstanding fee to the department of cardiothoracic surgery. If you run into any trouble doing that, just say that you spoke directly to me, Walter Katz, and that I approved the charge." He turned to Declan and asked, "Is there anything else I can do for you, Dec?"

"No. I think that about does it, Dr. Katz. I really appreciate you helping me keep my kneecaps intact."

"Good. I'll hear from you tomorrow at rounds." He turned and disappeared behind the shelves again.

Declan thanked the guy at the desk and made his way down the stairs. He felt an unexpected sense of satisfaction. That little transaction was not about the money. It was about respect and care. It was a telling gesture from a man whose professional stature essentially prevented him from being emotional. His gesture said more about how he felt toward his surgeons than anything else he would ever articulate to them directly.

The library courtyard was one level aboveground and overlooked the rose garden. Declan walked out the door and headed for the stairs that led down to the circular drive where he had parked his car. Just before going down, he could not avoid seeing the garden, in all its beauty, directly below him. He had not given it much thought for a few years now, until a different kind of rose caught his eye that day.

There, among the rose bushes, he saw Lauren. She was sitting on a bench, in her hospital pajamas, petting a cat. He stood still for a minute, not knowing what to do. In order to avoid the conglomeration of emotions that Lauren stirred up in him, he should have bypassed the stairs altogether and gone a different way to his car. Instead, an inexplicable impulse steered him toward the roses. In a flash, he thought about the debt Dr. Katz had just covered for him and hoped his good luck with the overdue books did not exact a higher price elsewhere. After this momentary hesitation, Declan started to make his way into the colorful garden.

The cat saw him first. It perked up but did not move from her arms. Declan stopped and grimaced as if he had done something wrong. He raised his hand to say hello but kept silent.

"I think you'll be okay, Dr. Baltierra. She is friendly. She was under a bush and came up to me as soon as I sat down."

"Have you been here long?" Dec sat on the bench's armrest, farthest from Lauren and the cat.

"I haven't really kept time. Maybe an hour."

"I'm glad you are enjoying the nice weather."

"Yes, it's great," she said.

"So, discharged on Monday—big day tomorrow. What are your plans?"

"I don't know. I haven't had any plans for over a year, really. You know…"

"Yes, of course," Dec said. "Do you have any family?"

"No," she immediately responded. Then she looked down at the cat, thoughtful. "I know I told the hospital people that I didn't. Mostly because I don't want my family to know what happened. Not that they would care much. They live in Victoria. I don't know how it works out with the hospital bills and all. I wouldn't want them to be involved. The lady from social services said that if I don't have anyone and own nothing, that I was lucky to have landed here because the state would pick up my bills. I'm pretty sure my brother and his wife would not want to have anything to do with me right now. The only other family I know of is an aunt who lives in Massachusetts. She used to come visit when my mother was still alive. I was just a little girl then, and she seemed to like me. I haven't seen her for a long time, though."

"Did social services offer you anything else?"

"Yes. Sort of. Apparently, there is a shelter here in Galveston. They also gave me phone numbers of places I could call for jobs and numbers for rehab centers here and in Houston."

As they continued to converse, the cat had climbed down from Lauren's arms and was now rubbing against Declan's leg. He scratched between its ears. The little creature seemed to like that. He and Lauren sat there watching it for a few moments, and then Declan made some observations about the different roses around them to fill the silence.

"How do you know so much about roses?" Lauren asked.

He told her about his mother's business. All along, his mind was simultaneously hard at work analyzing the situation. His conscience was navigating uncharted waters. He thought about offering to drive her all the way to Victoria and trying to talk her brother into helping her out. Maybe he could help her get in touch with that aunt and find out if she liked Lauren enough to take her in. He also thought about asking Sam to take her as an inpatient in the psychiatry department with the excuse that she needed more than group counseling. For a split second, he considered asking Abby for help. Would she allow a possibly unstable girl to stay with her for a while? He realized the magnitude of that stupid idea as soon as he had it.

In the end, all he could say was, "Have you had lunch?"

"No, not yet."

"Come on, it's my treat. I'm sure you haven't had real fast food in a while."

"Oh no, Doctor. I couldn't—"

"Everything in moderation, right?" He stood up and offered his hand.

With his help, she rose, but then timidly withdrew her hand from his. The cat was sitting on the bench watching them. She petted the furry animal one last time, and they both began to walk away. The cat followed them to the edge of the garden. They waved the kitty goodbye and made their way toward the main hospital complex.

Declan figured she could use an old-fashioned, greasy burger and fries. Besides, he was hungry.

"Let's go to the Shrine," he said.

They took a turn and walked half a block toward the Shriners Burns Hospital. The Shrine was a premier burn center and an impressive, state-of-the-art, architecturally beautiful hospital. Children from all over the world went there for care, mostly geared toward plastic and reconstructive surgery. The hospital's exterior was a combination of reddish-gray marble and glass. It connected with the main university hospital complex via a walkway five stories above the street. It was an amazing institution for children whose families never paid one cent for world-class specialized treatment. To the UTMB community, it was the best restaurant in town.

The Shrine's cafeteria was on the tenth floor and overlooked the entire island. The blue-green ocean stretched to the east as far as the eye could see. The view to the south was a picturesque spread of gingerbread houses from a bygone era. Galveston had been Texas's most important port and mercantile center during the nineteenth century. The island had endured wars, depression, and powerful hurricanes. Yet from high above, its old neighborhoods conserved a sense of unperturbed elegance.

Declan and Lauren continued to chat sporadically. He shared a bit of the history he had picked up over the years regarding some of the mansions and pointed them out in the matrix of streets. She made her own observations about the sights below.

"All my life I have been looking up," she said. "I tried to change that a year ago. I left my hometown for Houston, hoping my life would change for the better. I thought that maybe I would see life from a place like this—you know, from above. But as you know, I totally got lost and ended up looking up again from an even deeper hole. If only I could stay up here forever." She gazed at the ocean. "It's so pretty."

Declan didn't know how to reply.

After the meal, he said, "Well, I have to go, but you are welcome to stay here for as long as you want. Anybody here can point you back to the main hospital."

"No. I think I will go back to my room now," Lauren said.

"I will walk with you, then."

"You don't have to, Dr. Baltierra."

"I know."

As they crossed the glass walkway above the street, Declan saw the glimmer of his yellow car parked in front of the rose garden.

Unable to control itself, his mind came up with what should have been an irrational idea. What if he offered to have Lauren stay at his mother's home in Houston? He knew his mom wouldn't mind, and would actually be delighted to have some company. Additionally, Lauren needed a job, so she could work at the shop. One of their oldest employees had been an alcoholic, but he had overcome his problem years ago—Dec calculated about fifteen years sober. He was a good man who would likely be glad to take Lauren to his meetings. Also, Declan's vacation was coming up at the end of that week. He would have an entire month to give her a hand until she got back on her feet.

Surprised that this idea didn't actually sound completely crazy, he fumbled to find the best words to frame his suggestion.

"Lauren, you are welcome to stay at my house. I mean, not with me, but with my mother—in Houston. And a job at her shop. You know, until you get a better idea about where to go and what to do."

"Huh?" Lauren looked flabbergasted.

If she hadn't been expressive in the past, she was less so now. She simply had no answer. How could she respond? Did he pity her that much? Hadn't he already done enough for her? Could someone actually be this nice? Or was he nuts?

Declan inferred what was going through her mind. "It may sound as crazy for you to hear as it is for me to say it. But I mean it. It is a little…actually, it's a lot unorthodox, but I want you to think about it." He smiled and then added, "If you can decide before I come to my senses, though, it would be quite helpful."

When they reached her room, she sat on the bed staring at her fidgety hands on her lap. After a moment, he said, "Okay, then, I think I will go now. I will see you tomorrow, Lauren." He started to walk away.

"Dr. Baltierra," she exclaimed, lifting her head.

Declan stopped, turned around, and met her eyes. There was a wave of strange yet comfortable energy between them.

She said, "I would love and appreciate that very much."

"Good." His forehead puckered and he rubbed his chin. "Maybe the best thing is to check you out of here right now. I was actually on my way to see my mother when we met earlier in the garden. It would be a good opportunity to take you there. So, while you get dressed and gather your things, I'll go talk to your nurse and write a discharge order."

"I actually don't have anything to gather. I don't even have clothes to wear. All I have is this gown and these hospital shoes."

"Oh. Right. Give me a minute. I'll be right back."

Declan went out for about five minutes and then returned with a pair of surgical scrubs. He stepped out to allow her to change. Shortly after, she opened the door and looked at him shyly.

"You ready?" he asked.

"I think so."

Lauren waved goodbye to the nurses behind the workstation. They all seemed surprised and curious as the pair began to walk out of the ward. Her own nurse, Barbara, waved back, wiping quiet tears from her eyes. Lauren was touched by everyone's outpouring of emotion but held back her own tears. Despite a cursory apprehension, she felt an inkling of calm and reassurance to be leaving with Declan by her side. They walked away from the place and from the team that had helped her get a second chance at life.

Again, they went through the rose garden to get to his car. He opened the door for her and helped her ease into the seat.

Just before he closed it, they both noticed their cat friend had returned and was now sitting a few steps away on the curb, staring at them. Lauren looked at the creature as one looks at a loved one before leaving on a long trip. The scene made Declan feel a little sad. He wasn't sure what to do or say. There was a combination of something magical and comical about the cat that made him stall.

"Would you like to take the cat with us?" he asked.

"No, not at all. The last thing I want is to burden you and your mother with two strays. Besides, what if the poor animal has a family?" Lauren asked, a wistful tone in her voice. "She is just so friendly and pretty, that's all. I'm okay, really."

"I tell you what, Lauren. The cat does not have a collar, so it must not belong to anyone. I doubt it has any family because I have actually seen him or her—"

"I'm pretty sure it's a girl," she said.

"Okay, I've seen *her* around here alone for some time now, I just hadn't given it much thought. Let's open the back door, and if she gets in the car, we'll take her. Deal?"

Lauren got out, opened the back door, and jokingly asked the cat if she cared to come along. Surprisingly, the feline sauntered toward the car and jumped onto the back seat. Lauren kept the door open for a minute as both she and Declan stood in disbelief. They sort of expected the cat to at least give things a second thought. Instead, the cat jumped into the front and settled in the passenger's seat.

"There's our answer," he said. "She doesn't even want to share."

Lauren slipped into the seat and rearranged the cat on her lap. "Blossom. That's your name."

It was around two p.m. when, on that pleasantly sunny day, the three of them left the island together.

SIXTEEN

The homes on Morningside Drive were stately but far from lavish. Most had spacious lawns and landscaped gardens. Tall, leafy trees lined the sidewalks and shaded the manicured grass. The homes reflected architectural diversity—Capes, Tudor, classic Texan brick, and Spanish. A sense of effortless tidiness pervaded the neighborhood. Not one mailbox was rusted, and not one stood on a wooden or bent pole. These mailboxes had custom bases that matched the exterior of each home. Some lawns were fenced with wrought iron or white pickets. No chain link in sight.

Many homes on the street had ample windows that provided a view into people's living rooms. It was through such a window that Declan's mother saw the yellow Mercedes turn into the driveway of her red-tiled, Spanish-style house. She had been sitting at the dining room table paging through *Better Homes & Gardens*. Usually she would have taken her glasses off and rushed out of the house to welcome Declan. Noticing that her son was not alone, she hung back and waited until they got out of the car. She couldn't make out the unknown woman's face.

"A cat?" Mrs. Baltierra asked herself when she saw Dec take Blossom in one hand and help Lauren out of the seat with the other. Declan was showing off some of the landmarks of the neighborhood—the old oak tree in the front lawn, the thick vines of red hibiscus they'd smuggled from their home in Mexico and which now formed a courtly arch over the driveway. He also pointed to the house across the street where his academic archrival in high school, now a physics professor at MIT, used to live. Then she saw them turn toward the house. Just before opening the front door, she looked through the peephole and noticed that the cat had leaped from Dec's arm and was exploring the immaculately trimmed front yard. Most of all, she noticed how Declan, standing with his hands deep in the pockets of his worn-out Levi's, glanced at the unpretentious, unmade, and mysterious woman in scrubs.

Lauren had walked over to retrieve the cat and was spending a few seconds rubbing Blossom's upturned belly. Mrs. Baltierra smiled with a peculiar air of certainty, instantly realizing that whomever this person happened to be, she was *the one*—even if her son didn't know it yet.

"Hi, Dec," she said as she walked calmly down the front steps.

"Hey, Mom." He gave her a peck on the cheek.

"I thought you'd get here earlier?"

"I know. But as you can see, there is a reason. Come on, meet Lauren and Blossom."

"Who is who?"

Lauren straightened. "Oh, I'm Lauren. The cat is…"

"Blossom," Mrs. Baltierra finished as she bent over to pick up the cat. "You are a playful little thing, aren't you? Well, you are in luck, because we are all eating turkey."

Wide-eyed, the cat stared back at Declan's mother as if she'd understood what was said.

"She likes you, Mom."

"That's because I said *turkey*. All cats know when something good is coming their way, huh, Bloss?" She turned to Lauren. "Do you guys work together?"

Immediately, Declan said, "Mom, why don't we take it inside and talk over dinner." Then he glanced reassuringly at Lauren.

"Of course, let's step inside." She passed Blossom on to Declan, placed her arm under Lauren's, and led her in. "Lauren, welcome home."

Declan went back to the car to retrieve the litter box and other cat essentials they had stopped to purchase on their way from Galveston.

"Bloss, you and Lauren will be just fine," he told the cat.

He went into the kitchen, but nobody was there. His mother was giving Lauren a tour of the house. Declan set up the litter box in the mudroom just off the kitchen. After that, he placed the feeding and drinking bowls on the kitchen island, onto which the cat jumped and sat placidly, observing her new surroundings. Declan coaxed her to eat or drink, to no avail.

"Suit yourself," he said and then went over to the stove to look under the foil, which covered a couple of serving plates. The aromas reawakened his appetite.

"Dec, instead of snooping around, you can go ahead and start serving," his mother said, surprising him from behind.

"Where is Lauren?"

"She is changing into something more apt for dinner."

"Mom, with regard to—"

"Dec, don't worry about it. From the moment she looked at me with the same eyes I used to see in the mirror after Dad died, and when I realized that she quite literally only had those scrubs on, I knew Lauren was here to stay. I know there must be a good reason and a sensible story behind all this. But if she is to begin shedding that forsaken aura about her, we should make her first meal with us as amenable and as far removed from whatever is bothering her. It seems you are trying to help her, and I want to be part of that. For now, let's spend time on more lighthearted subjects. I'll learn what this is all about in due time."

"Thanks, Mom."

"You are welcome. I will call you about it tonight."

"Okay."

"Great, bring the lemonade from the fridge. We'll eat outside on the deck."

"Sounds good. By the way, we had a meal not too long ago, but Lauren didn't eat much," he said.

The deck overlooked a suburban paradise. A white brick fence awash in green ivy hemmed in the garden. Except for the hibiscus to the right, colorful roses were everywhere. The roses lined a small bridge that arched across the swimming pool, surrounded the small gazebo at the far corner, and hung from each level of a functioning white stone fountain to the far left of the garden.

Lauren fit perfectly into a pair of Mrs. Baltierra's casual khakis, a simple peach-colored cotton tank top, and a new pair of white Keds. Mrs. Baltierra gestured to have her join them outside.

"I see you found something that fit. How do the shoes feel?"

"Oh, just fine. Thank you. Thank you very much."

"Everything is served, Lauren, please take a seat," Declan said while on his feet.

They sat, and after the first bite of the turkey, Lauren's eyes widened. "Mrs. Baltierra, this is very good. You are a great cook."

Declan raised an eyebrow at his mother. She smiled back at Lauren. "Honey, it's called Eatzi's—the best take-out place in Houston. As my son here will agree, the one thing I am not is a good cook. Perhaps you noticed that the kitchen looks as good as new—"

"Because it is," Declan finished.

Bright and casual conversation continued. Blossom's curiosity about the extra plate on the table became too great. She soon jumped up and sampled her share of the turkey.

"It appears she has officially joined the family," Mrs. Baltierra said, glancing at Declan.

"I hope she also eats cat food," he replied matter-of-factly.

Innately, Declan knew that his mother's glance and comment might not have simply referred to Blossom.

The evening went on with more tours of the garden and the house. They played a game of Chinese checkers, which Lauren won. They made a trip to the pet store and retrieved supplies that Declan's mother deemed more appropriate. These included premium organic food, a tall cat condo, toys, and a self-cleaning electric litter box. They gave Lauren a quick tour of nearby neighborhoods. As soon as they returned home, it was time for Declan to head back to Galveston.

Lauren held the cat in her arms and stood by the front door next to Mrs. Baltierra, who had told Declan she would take good care of the two girls. Just as he opened his car door, Lauren walked a few steps forward and said, "Dr. Baltierra, thank you. Thank you for—for everything."

"You are welcome. I will be in touch. Goodbye for now."

SEVENTEEN

A week had passed since Declan had dropped off Lauren at his mother's, and now his one-month vacation was beginning. It was Saturday morning, and Declan was once again on I-45 toward Houston. He thought about work and mentally rechecked items he'd completed before leaving Dr. Katz at the reins. Henry, John, and Tiny, to their relief, were moving on to other rotations. They would've hated to work on that surgical service with anyone other than Declan.

Nurses on the sixth floor had regarded Declan with peculiar affection throughout the week. Lauren's day-shift nurse was the only one who had directly asked him how she was doing.

"Just fine for now," he'd answered.

The nurse had seemed content with his reply, or at least she didn't ask for further details. The boys had obviously gotten word of the unusual situation too. Except for Tiny, the crew did not push Declan on the subject. They knew that no matter what the specifics were, he'd be doing or trying to do the right thing.

"Dec, I'm not sure whether to add or subtract points from your surgical stud score," Tiny had said while trailing him through the surgical ward. "I know there is no way in hell I'd do what you did. It's—how do I put it? Weird, but nice." Heaving slightly, he finally caught up with Declan. "Dude, you don't have her stashed away in your shitty apartment against her will, do you?"

"No."

"Well, where is she, man? What did you do? Give me some material." Declan didn't answer. "You are not going to talk about it, are you?"

"Not with you."

"Man, is this legal?" Tiny had continued.

"What? Helping out a patient outside the hospital, or your not knowing the details about it?"

"You know sooner or later I'll get wind of everything."

"I know," Dec had said. "But in the meantime, let's take care of some patients."

Indeed, he had left everything in order. As he reached the outskirts of Houston, he realized it was safe to leave work behind and look forward to his time off. Unlike vacation periods before this, though, he felt nervous about the days ahead. His break was now immutably entwined with Lauren. Dec felt a certain responsibility to help her get back on her feet, but he didn't have a specific plan on how to do it.

His mother had given him a few updates during the week. They had spent most of Monday afternoon and evening shopping—procuring Lauren a wardrobe, of course. Lauren had begun group therapy on Wednesday, and she was spending the rest of the time learning the art of flower arranging. Despite the lack of a real plan, things were going well. So, rather than trying to reach for intelligent thoughts regarding the situation, he turned off the AC, lowered the windows, and allowed the warm Gulf air to beat into the car. He popped in an old Springsteen tape from the glove box and, without really registering the words in his mind, sang "Born in the USA," "Hungry Heart," "Dancing in the Dark," and "Human Touch" at the top of his lungs.

While traffic was not as heavy as during the workweek, the usual bottleneck at the junction of I-45 and US Route 59 slowed him down. Flanked by large eighteen-wheelers and enveloped by the smell of diesel, he took refuge in the loud music. As soon as the traffic eased up, he turned onto Kirby Drive toward Le Peep, one of his all-time favorite brunch restaurants a few blocks from home. This would allow him to gather his thoughts and make some plans for his vacation over a perfectly browned waffle with fresh strawberries and whipped cream.

The clientele was mostly a combination of professionals and older, well-heeled folks. With his hair in windblown but dashing disarray, Declan sat at a table and began to read the sports section of the *Chronicle.* As had happened on similar occasions before, he was coerced into making small talk with a flirtatious waitress.

"May I get you another cup of coffee?" she asked.

"Too much caffeine makes me a little crazy," he responded.

"In that case, let me leave the whole pot here for you."

"That would be dangerous," he said.

"Can I get you anything else? And I really do mean *anything.*"

"I think I am okay, thanks."

"All right, then." She puckered her lips and spun off.

"Honey, I think that girl is toying with you," said a refined older lady sitting alone at a table across from him.

He turned to face the elderly woman. "You noticed too, huh?"

"Yes. And I tell you what. I don't blame her. If I was about a hundred years younger, I'd be giving it a shot myself." She winked.

"Thank you, ma'am," Dec replied graciously.

"So, what does a debonair young man like you, without a ring—don't think I didn't notice—do for a living that keeps him from being accompanied to a Saturday brunch?"

"Well, what does a beautiful woman like yourself do for a living that keeps her unaccompanied in a joint like this too?" he volleyed back with a grin.

"Touché. And thank you. I am a rich old dame whose husband hasn't punched out from work at Marathon Oil since the end of the Korean War." She gave a slight shrug and smiled.

"That's amazing dedication."

"Depends on how you look at it," she said.

"I know. I actually meant to say that your dedication to him is amazing." Dec raised his coffee cup to salute her.

"I like you already. So, I'm going to burden you with my little story." She took a sip of coffee, and after a gentle sigh, she seemed to extract her next words from the deep confines of her mind.

"We met in the Philippines. He was in the Army Corps of Engineers, and I was an MP. I know, rare for girls in those days to be military police, but they were trying it out. His R&R with a few of his buddies got a bit too rowdy one night. We got called in to see about the situation. And instead of me apprehending him, to make a long story short, we eventually 'apprehended' each other. Needless to say, we got hitched soon after. Following the war, he found and eventually also married a very lucrative job here. Ever since, I still sit in places like this, alone. You see, I haven't been able to fall out of love with him, despite his other 'marriage.' Sometimes I wish it had actually been another woman—some skanky type who would have made it simple for me to leave. But in his own distant way, he has always loved me too. It has been a long, odd bond between us, but a bond nonetheless.

"In answer to your question, then, a woman like me hangs out in joints like this because I can't help but share my husband with his job. And of course, to make conversation with good-looking young men like you."

"Well, then, a guy like me sits around in joints like this to listen to ladies like yourself," Dec offered.

"Oh, sort of like a gigolo," she said with a smirk.

At that moment, the waitress had returned to fill their coffee cups and stood there waiting to hear what Declan had to say in reply.

"No, not quite like a gigolo. More like a doctor," he said.

"I knew it. Are you sure there is nothing else I can do for you, Doctor?" the waitress said with a teasing wink.

"I'm sure," he answered with a polite nod.

"Hmm." The waitress sighed disappointedly and retired to the kitchen.

"Oh yes. Busy doctor. Little time for gals like that," the older lady said.

"I suppose so."

"Son, let me tell you. No matter what you do or who you are, make sure that at some point you have someone to fill that chair in front of you at brunch time. It's the only thing that matters. Even if—as in my case—it only happens once in a blue moon." The old lady smiled at Declan and then turned away to take another sip of her coffee.

"Thank you, ma'am. I enjoyed our conversation," he told her.

"Rather one-sided, but me too. Please carry on with your meal and don't mind me."

Declan finished eating and took care of his bill. He wished the elderly woman a good day and headed for the door. His car was parked outside, facing the spot where he'd just sat. Through the window, he saw the empty table and the old lady still sipping coffee across from it. In a flash, he pictured himself sharing brunch with Lauren. He shook his head to clear it, and headed to his mother's.

He had a key to the house, but he always rang first. The cleaning lady opened the door. Tita had been working for them for many years—she was older and loyal, and a good friend to his mother. "Declan, come in. Sorry everything is upside down, but you know—cleaning."

"I know, Tita. No problem."

"Oh, you got laundry? Here, I take care of it."

"No, you don't have to do that. I'll do it myself."

"No, no, here, give it to me. You can't do it. You gonna mix it all up like you always do. Look at that shirt you are wearing. It's faded and ugly. Here!" She snapped the laundry sack from Declan's arm and continued scolding. "I have been washing your trousers since you were a little kid. I'm not gonna stop now. Okay?"

Realizing he had lost that battle, he surrendered the laundry and gave her a hug.

"Your mother and that girl—"

"Lauren."

"Okay, that Lauren. They are at the shop." Tita shrugged.

"And Blossom?"

"What?" Tita said with a confused look.

"The cat?"

"Yes, yes. The cat. The cat is also at the shop. Wherever they go, the cat goes too." She shook her head in disbelief.

"Good!"

"Not so good for me. I have never seen so many hairs all over this house in my life."

"I'm sorry, Tita. That's what happens when you have pets."

"We would not have a cat and all the hairs and stuff if—"

"Tita, come on," he pleaded with her, playfully, following her to the laundry room.

"Okay, okay. I just—I still don't know what to think. Your mother tells me she is a guest. I don't know. What kind of guest? You know?" She was prodding for more information. She was not suspicious or unsympathetic—Tita honestly cared for Declan and his mother in a grandmotherly way.

"No, I don't know, actually. But she's important to me." He cocked his head analytically. "You know, I think I will head up to my room now."

"Okay. I finish cleaning," she said and turned on the vacuum. She adopted an air of satisfied pride, as if he'd explained everything to her.

Just like his mom a week before, Tita felt that she knew something he didn't.

—m—

Declan's room had not changed since he had traded it for his college dorm many years ago. It was as spartan as he'd left it. A black bedspread covered his full-size bed. His desk, opposite the bed, held an old computer and printer. The wall behind the bed had a traditional blue-and-white banner with the inscription *For God, for Country and for Yale.* A picture of himself at ten years of age, in football gear, flanked by his parents, hung on the wall above his desk. Under the large window, which faced the garden, was his old stereo and TV. He turned on the stereo and played a Ray Conniff LP that had belonged to his father. Then he stood in front of the desk and contemplated the photograph from so many years ago.

He had been the star fullback for the Buffalos of the Colegio Francés Hidalgo—his elementary school back in Mexico. The uniform matched, exactly, that of the NFL's Buffalo Bills. That day, they had defeated the boys from the rival Colegio Tepeyac. Declan had scored two touchdowns and could see and feel his dad's overwhelming sense of pride for his performance. His mother, as usual, had made arrangements for Kool-Aid, sandwiches, and cookies for the team to enjoy after the game.

He remembered that day as vividly as if he were still there. Declan could still hear loud cheers and see many happy faces all around him. He recalled the camaraderie of his teammates when they huddled up to celebrate their win. He never forgot the cool touch of the trophy as it passed through his hands, and he could still smell the foul yet oddly gratifying combination of sweat, dirt, and the foamy material of protective gear. Above all, he remembered the bright blue sky under which all that happiness had taken place—the last day his dad ever saw him play.

The LP ended. Declan snapped out of the past and saw himself from a distance, in his old bedroom, in the present.

He had no plan and no goals in regard to Lauren. And once again, he opted not to think about it too much. For the moment, he would just address the Lauren situation one day at a time. He went downstairs and waved goodbye to Tita.

The Petal Inc. was located in the shopping center across from the exclusive Galleria mall. It wasn't far from the Westin, where he and Abby had spent a night not too long ago. He transiently looked at the high rise hotel at a distance and took a slow, deep breath in. *No regrets*, he told himself. He let the breath out and turned into a parking lot off Westheimer Road. Tucked in the corner opposite FAO Schwarz was the business that had made his career possible. Just inside was a black marble fountain with an abundant flower display on the top. The front area of the store was filled with mostly contemporary arrangements, catering to yuppie types and to the various hotels in the area. In the central portion of the shop, a few steps down, was an exhaustive display of flowers inside and outside the refrigerators. Display stands featured baskets, cards, stuffed animals, chocolates, candles, and plants. Just beyond the customer service desk, a narrow archway led to the work areas and to an office in the back.

Most of the customers were shopping in the central part of the store—the heart of the business, which as usual, was brisk. But only a handful of people were looking around the front area, and among these was a man in a suit who looked lost.

"Is there anything I can help you with?" Declan asked him.

"Do you work here?"

"I do."

"I don't know. I guess I'm just browsing," the man said.

"What's the occasion?" Dec inquired.

"Fortieth anniversary."

"Wow. Congratulations!"

"Thank you," the gentleman replied.

"Are you planning anything besides flowers?"

"I haven't planned anything yet. I know our kids are throwing us a party next weekend. But you know, I want to do something special for her...I've already bought her a nice piece of jewelry. I guess I want to somehow incorporate flowers with it. And I was told this was the best place to get them. I want the best, no matter how much it costs. For example, how much is this?" The man pointed to an elegant arrangement of birds-of-paradise and purple tiger lilies in a black Japanese-style vase.

"Well, I'd have to look it up," Declan said, "but honestly, that's the sort of thing you would find on the Marriott's reception desk. I don't know you, but what really counts in this case is the situation, the atmosphere." Declan's voice slipped into the non-chalance of a seasoned salesman, sincere and friendly, just like old times. "If you don't have concrete plans, let me suggest the following: You and your wife arrive at the world-class Houstonian Hotel on the night of your choosing. The valet takes your car, and the two of you proceed to the grand dining room. As soon as you give your name, an attendant shows you to a table where a bottle of champagne is already chilled and subsequently served to you." The man was hooked, picturing the scene, and Declan leaned closer. "A live jazz ensemble accompanies a five-course meal that you have chosen in advance. Someone is monitoring and ensuring a high level of pampering and service throughout the meal. After a dance or two, or at a time of your preference, another fellow brings out a long and beautiful box containing forty roses, as well as the piece of jewelry you had planned to give your wife. After she is awed by the latter, the attendant congratulates the two of you on your anniversary, and in less than five minutes, he expertly arranges the roses in a vase that is delivered to your wife the next day—at your hotel room if you wish to stay the night or at your home." He stepped back and shrugged. "But then again, that is just an idea."

"Sounds pretty good. Is this really something you can arrange for me?"

"Absolutely!"

"And I thought you just sold flowers here," the man said, astonished.

"Well, more than that, we sell *moments in life*," Dec said. "If you'd just wanted flowers, I would have directed you to the appropriate section of the nearest grocery store."

"Yes, I can see that." The man smiled.

"Here, you can talk to that blond lady over there." Dec pointed to and waved to Rhonda, one of their longtime employees. She waved back from behind one of the displays on the center court and acknowledged the gentleman. "She will make all the arrangements you want and give you even more options, if you wish."

"Thank you very much, young man."

"You are welcome, sir."

Declan felt like he was back in the swing of things. Despite his profession, he could still come back to the flower business, talk to people, and not only make a sale but also truly help someone—invariably affluent—make the best of their particular occasion.

Declan exchanged hugs and handshakes with the employees who, by now, were old friends. He learned that his mother was a few miles away at the warehouse and that Lauren was in the back with Willie, making flower arrangements. Willie was in his sixties and had been sober for many years. Declan's mother had said Willie had already introduced Lauren to his therapy group and, as Declan had hoped, taken her under his wing.

As Declan walked through the archway to the back, Blossom rubbed up against his leg. He reached down and picked her up. He headed to the large workbench full of flowers.

"Hey, guys, how's it going?"

"Dec! It's a pleasure seeing you again," Willie said.

Lauren was sitting next to Willie, learning the process of making an arrangement to decorate a church for a wedding. She looked delighted to see him.

"Dr. Baltierra," she said warmly with a budding smile.

EIGHTEEN

"Hey, hey, hey! Where are you going?"

"I am just putting on more tea."

"Oh. I thought you might be heading to bed," Frank said.

"No, I wouldn't leave you hanging like that, hon. By the way, please put the box on the table. You're holding on to it again. I don't want you to drop it."

"Huh. I wonder if it would break," he joked.

"Frank, don't make me hurt you. Here, give it to me." I took it and placed it safely on the counter. Our dog had not moved an inch and remained asleep under the table. Even before the water boiled, Frank was insisting that I sit down and finish the story.

"Babe, let's go. It looks to me like you are just at the beginning."

I dropped new tea bags in our cups and poured the hot water. I grabbed us a small container of butter cookies and sat back down. Frank was almost correct with his last statement.

More than *the* beginning, though, this point in the story was *their* beginning. So, I continued.

"Can I help?" Declan asked Willie and Lauren.

"Of course. Lauren and I just finished the corsages and boutonnieres for a wedding at the Adam's Mark. Tony and Linda are at the hotel working on the centerpieces. We still need a couple of big arrangements for the church," Willie said.

"Man, you are cutting it close. When's the wedding?" Declan asked.

"It's a late one. Six o'clock. Just down the road on Westheimer," Willie answered.

"Okay, then." Declan looked at the choice of flowers on the table. "I guess it's the standard gladiola and white roses in a white plastic vase."

"Your mother tried to talk them into something classier, but they wouldn't hear of it. Understandable, though. The couple is about my age. To their credit, they had very old-fashioned but precise requirements for what they wanted."

"Fine. Standard it is," Declan said.

"Now that you are here and since you don't look like you'll be operating anytime soon, I'm going to go get some lunch." Willie got up from the stool with a groan. "I was thinking about something from Souper Salad. What will it be for you two?"

"I just had brunch," Declan answered.

"Lauren?"

"Oh, I'm fine, thank you," she said.

"You haven't eaten all morning, and we still have a ways to go. And Dec, I know that whatever half-edible thing I put in front of you, you will eat. So, salads and sandwiches it is." Willie walked away, rendering them unable to protest.

"Willie is such a character," Declan said.

"Yes. He's great." Lauren suddenly lost a bit of her ease.

Declan sensed her apprehension, but he knew there wasn't much he could do about it except to be his usual, friendly self.

"How do you like the flower business?" Declan asked her as he gave Blossom one last pat on the head and lowered her onto the worktable. Once on four paws again, Blossom went straight to Lauren.

Lauren broke into a smile. "I love it. And I thank you for it. For everything—"

"Hey, I know. But please, no more thank-yous. It's not charity. Otherwise, we'll both feel awkward about it." He wondered how much he believed what he was saying. "Perhaps we should just think of our relationship, you know, all this, as friends giving each other a hand. I mean, this is nothing out of the ordinary. It's about people helping people with no strings attached. It's about getting you back on your feet and on a life course that you're excited about. It's about you not ever feeling like you owe us anything. It's about me doing what my family taught me to do. It's about running into each other in the future and doing a high five, knowing we are just ordinary friends, even if we started out from an extraordinary situation. So, here, give me five and let's finish these flowers." Declan raised his hand out over the table. Lauren's met his halfway.

They both smiled and gathered materials from the shelves. As they worked, despite his previous words, both had a distinctive, introspective conviction that their relationship wasn't now and never would be ordinary. In fact, Lauren's thoughts were a silent recital of two key words: *relationship* and *friendship*. She suddenly felt ignorant about what these words meant—in general and for both of them.

Lauren was still learning, so she told Dec she would follow his lead. Copying his every move and only a few steps behind him, she began the systematic yet creative process of making the arrangements. They cut blocks of foam to fit the large white vases. They secured the blocks with tape. The next step was to fill the vases with enough warm water to saturate the foam while keeping the vase about three-quarters full. This process allowed the foam to become a pliable yet strong foundation to hold the assorted stems in place. Once this was done, they began to insert gladiolas into the foam in a fan-shaped configuration, followed by progressively smaller fans of roses. The roses were not only different shades of white but also different sizes, ending with vines of miniature white roses for the bottom layer, trailing down over the top edge of the vases. Finally, they adorned all the gaps between the flowers with ivy and filled the space behind the gladiola background with fern. They were finished—with the first two of six arrangements. They carried the two completed vases to a stand next to the worktable and stood back to admire their creations.

"Not too shabby, huh?"

"They look great," Lauren said.

"I guess I still have the touch," Declan said.

They made their way back to the worktable. Without looking at Declan, Lauren gathered the materials for the next set of arrangements. "I think it's interesting how you can do stuff like this, as well as the complicated things you do as a doctor. I mean, not in terms of physical ability, because if you can operate on a heart, this is, like, nothing. It's hard to picture you, someone like you, working in a back room like this making flower arrangements." Smiling, she shook her head.

Declan also smiled but didn't say anything.

She continued, "The whole time I was in the hospital—well, when I was conscious, anyway—I heard all the people who helped take care of me say great things about you. I mean everyone, from the doctors who worked under you to my nurses and therapists and even the cleaning crews. I still sort of do. People here really like you. The picture I've had of you is of some godly figure—I don't know. It's just hard to imagine—to see that you're like, you know, a normal person."

"Gee, thanks. I think."

"No, I don't mean that." Lauren started to redden.

"What you really mean to say is that you can't imagine that Declan here puts his pants on one leg at a time, like the rest of us," Willie said. He strode in with a couple of brown take-out bags. Rhonda and Sallie followed with sodas, paper plates, and utensils.

"Honey, Willie is right," Rhonda said. "He wasn't always Dr. Baltierra. Granted, he was always a little different. He was very smart, and we were constantly hearing about how he did this and that great thing in high school. Always winning medals and everything. But even back then, he was totally into this business. Believe it or not, he is the one who hired me. He gave me the rundown of the business, which was much smaller then, and it was basically out of a warehouse in west Houston. I still remember this young, snot-nosed kid—well, not snot-nosed—but young. He always wore this dirty baseball cap and the same T-shirt full of holes when flower shipments came in. After that, quite often, you'd see him completely exhausted, sleeping in the back of his mom's van or on some corner of the warehouse floor. Anyway, he always was and always will be one of us."

"Yeah, and he didn't even want to be a doctor then," Sallie said. "His uncle would often take him on his rounds at the hospital, but Declan always insisted that he was going to study business and make this into a flower empire. In fact, he had a full scholarship to the undergraduate business program at UT Austin, a school he loved more than anything. I guess some counselor twisted his arm into applying to Ivy League schools. And not surprisingly, he got into all of them. It really shocked all of us when he chose one of those over the Longhorns. I guess something happened in college that changed his mind about what he wanted to study. And many years later, like Willie said, Declan became Dr. Baltierra."

"Here, though, he's just Dec," Willie added.

"Wow!" Declan said. "I'm surprised you guys didn't go into the things that are really embarrassing. Believe me, Lauren, these guys are ruthless."

"Oh yes, we are. But don't worry, we have lots of time to expand on the really juicy stuff." Rhonda winked at Lauren.

When they finished their lunch break, Rhonda said, "Dec, Kate is supervising two other wedding jobs at the warehouse and wanted me to check the detail for this wedding at the hotel. Since you are not a doctor right now, I was wondering if you could take care of that for me. It's pretty busy today, so I would rather stick around to help with things out front."

"Sure, no problem."

"Here is the paperwork. It's at the Adam's Mark down the street. I think you should take Lauren. This will allow her to see that side of the business. Willie and Sallie can finish up the church arrangements. By the way"—she pointed to the vases on the stand—"those turned out perfect."

"Thanks," Dec said. "Lauren, what do you say? Wanna go check it out?"

"Yes. But…" Lauren hesitated, looking around.

"But nothing," Rhonda said. "I know Blossom is in the lounge. I saw her there when I went in to get more soda. We'll keep an eye on her."

"Speaking of the cat, how is she doing?" Declan asked as they started to walk through the shop toward the front door.

"Just fine. She really loves it here and at your mother's house. She especially loves riding in the car. Blossom is very well behaved."

"Not bad for a stray cat from Galveston," he said. "By the way, after the stories you heard from the folks back there, you can call me Dec."

"I don't know. Your mom also wants me to call her Kate, but it feels odd, I don't know," Lauren confessed.

"What do you mean? Lauren, from the moment we left Galveston, you've come not only into a family, but like I said before, also to a good set of friends. Besides, I feel weird to be called doctor outside of work and especially around here. Also, you should know that my mother really likes it when people call her Kate," Declan explained.

"Okay, I will try."

"Good," Declan said as he opened the door for her.

Once again, they walked out into the bright Texas sky as they had done one week earlier—together.

NINETEEN

At the end of the day, Kate Baltierra took Blossom home and waited for Declan and Lauren to return. She spent some time playing with the cat before she heard Declan honk from the street.

The three of them met Rhonda and her partner at Pappadeaux Seafood Kitchen, just a few minutes from home. Dinner was pleasant, and Lauren kept up her end of the conversation. She teased Declan and got a laugh all around. She was referring to the strange face he made as he dug into three pounds of extra-spicy, Cajun-seasoned crawfish with his bare hands—all while sporting a white plastic bib.

After dinner, they took in a showing of *The Phantom of the Opera* in Houston's downtown arts district. Declan and Kate spent part of the ride home telling Lauren how the show compared to those they had seen in New York and San Francisco. Lauren didn't quite catch all the details, but she was happy to hear their analysis of the show—the fact that she saw a Broadway-caliber musical was a first and plenty spectacular for her.

Promptly after arriving home, Kate excused herself and retired to her bedroom. Lauren felt an awkward sensation, now that she was alone downstairs with Declan. She thanked Declan for a wonderful day, made her way to her bedroom, and proceeded to have a mentally unsettling night.

Since her first day there, Lauren had enjoyed the tranquility of having Blossom on the pillow next to her. But that night, the cat opted for *Saturday Night Live* downstairs with Declan. Now, there were too many things on her mind. The day's events kept flashing before her closed eyes like a movie trailer. She tried to order them and interpret their meaning. More importantly, her mind struggled with the chronic, self-deprecating uncertainty of how and even if she really fit into all these dreamlike yet wonderful episodes.

Declan had introduced her to the events coordinator at the hotel as one of Petal Inc.'s new designers. The rest of the team always included her in the work being done at the site. They even asked her opinion—on everything from whether a flower was out of place to if she thought the designs adhered to the work order. It gave Lauren an alien sense of belonging—not only to the group but also to the work itself. A feeling of creative freedom energized her as the day progressed. She felt joy and a sense of responsibility. She felt a natural affinity for the tasks asked of her. These tasks earned her and the group great praise from the hotel staff when all was said and done.

Lauren also thought about the relationship between Rhonda and her partner, Suzanne. She realized how limited her experiences and her vision had been in the past. They gave her a new feeling of hope as she saw the two of them interact in the warmest and most loving way.

And then there was Christine, Raoul, and the Phantom. She missed a few bits of dialogue here and there. But the images of Christine and Raoul pledging their love on the roof of the Paris Opera House obviated the need to nab every word. Lauren was mesmerized during the show but not until that night, alone, in the dark, did she feel comfortable enough to break down in tears. She could still hear "The Music of the Night" and trembled at the flashbacks of the explosive chandelier scene. She had been engrossed in the Phantom's wrath and power. In the end, she understood that his actions were the product of a love tainted by the scars he chose to hide behind his mask. Perhaps it was this similarity to her own life—a notion that she might be someone horrible, capable of love but restricted by the scars on her body and in her mind. That, at last, helped her cry herself to sleep.

—⁓—

Click!

Declan opened one eye after hearing the annoying sound of his mother's camera shutter. It was picture-perfect. He had fallen asleep on the couch in a slightly contorted position, facedown, with Blossom sprawled on his back.

"I can't believe the cat didn't move," Kate said in awe.

"Mom, I'm on vacation." Declan moaned as he slowly got up and stretched to a sitting position. Reluctantly, Blossom was forced to jump off.

"Which is why I take so much pride and pleasure in waking you up. As I always say, you may be a hotshot down in Galveston, but here you are my dish-washing, trash-collecting, bed-making son."

"You are cruel and most definitely not my favorite person right now."

"I know." Kate smiled, her index finger pointing around him. "Please make sure you clean up this little mess of yours and take Lauren out for a nice breakfast. I have a day of boring errands."

"You don't really have film in that camera, do you?"

"Yes, I do. I thought I would develop it and send it to that large, funny intern of yours." Kate grinned mischievously.

In a failed attempt to sound commanding, he said, "Blossom, attack that woman at once." Blossom replied with a huge, teeth-baring yawn.

It was only about eight in the morning, so he stretched out on the couch and went back to sleep.

By ten o'clock, a sliver between the blinds on the bay window let in way too much light. Declan was forced to get up. He darted to the kitchen and began to rummage for food. After touch-testing a handful of apples, he finally decided on a banana. As he peeled and took the first bite, he noticed that Lauren and the cat were both outside, on the bridge above the pool.

"Hey, how is it going?" He stuck his head out the door. "I have orders to take you out for breakfast."

"I appreciate that," she said. "But I just stole some fruit from the kitchen. I wanted to make you some breakfast, but I didn't want to make noise and wake you up."

"And of course, there was nothing in the fridge anyway, right?"

"Yes, that too," she replied with a smile.

"Well, are you hungry?"

"Honestly, I feel a tiny bit full," she said.

Declan thought for a second. Then he asked her if she would be interested in going for a run and grabbing brunch afterward. "Memorial Park is this nice little forest in the middle of Houston with a great running track. There are lots of people at this time, and it's a lot of fun."

"You think I can run?" Lauren asked, pointing to her chest.

"By now you should be able to do whatever you want."

"Maybe I'll just walk and wait for you," she suggested.

While she really wanted to run side by side with him, Lauren was afraid of not being able to keep up and was too embarrassed to tell him she did not have a sports bra. By this time, Declan was also on the bridge and had picked up the cat.

"Great, let's go," he said.

As previously planned, once at the park, Lauren walked along the track while Declan jogged. He went around the track six times—about three miles. He said hello every time he passed Lauren. Many of the people there were young college students, but there were quite a few families out for a quintessential day at the park. Some jogged or walked, some played Frisbee, some chased their dogs, others were chased by their dogs, some played tennis, and others played with children on the playground. The weather was hot and humid, but tolerable. On his last lap, Dec told Lauren he would meet her at the Water Stand. This was a mobile unit whose owner capitalized on the clientele to sell over-priced refreshments. Nice patio chairs with umbrellas, however, were provided at no extra charge.

"Hey, you didn't have to," he said as Lauren offered him a cold bottle of Evian.

"Oh yes, I did. You look like you have lost this and two other bottles' worth of water." Dec's shirt was dripping with sweat.

"Well, thank you."

"You are welcome," she said, thinking of how good it made her feel to spend some of her recently earned money on him, even if it was something as small as bottled water. She felt incredible satisfaction to hear him thank her.

"Okay, last thing. You are going to help me do some sit-ups."

They walked over to a spot under one of the many trees. He plopped down butt-first on the grass, bent his knees, and said, "All you gotta do is step on my sneakers and keep me from lifting my legs."

"I think I can do that," she said.

As soon as he made the first effort to sit up, he catapulted Lauren off and she fell flat on the ground. He sprang up and knelt beside her.

"Are you okay?"

"I guess I'm just a weakling." She laughed. "Maybe we should try it with me leaning against the tree for support."

Declan helped her up, and with her back braced against the tree, they tried again. He was able to get in two sets of fifty sit-ups.

"Wow. That's a lot," she observed.

"Well, not nearly enough. I used to be able to do a lot more, back when I was younger and firmer." He laughed. "And even with these few, I'll surely pay for it with a sore belly tomorrow."

"I'm sure you'll be fine."

"We'll see," he said. "Now, what I really need is a shower. I'm hideous."

"Oh yeah?" Lauren grinned and squirted Declan with her water bottle.

He squirted her back, and then it was a war, running and ducking around the tree, until the water ran out. Worn out, both soon lay down in the shade. After a few minutes, Declan got up and helped Lauren to her feet. They walked to his car and dried off with towels he kept in the trunk.

"You cheated. Your bottle was much larger," she said.

"Hey, you got it for me. What was I supposed to do?"

"Yes, I guess."

They headed back home, beaming.

Once home, they cleaned up and dressed in shorts, T-shirts, and sneakers. Declan could not help but notice that despite her clothes' simplicity, Lauren looked radiant.

Brunch was at the Galleria. This would allow Declan to have a smorgasbord of choices from the food court, and it would allow Lauren to purchase a sports bra and some sturdier running shoes. They settled on La Madeleine, a not-so-fast-food restaurant with a great selection of sandwiches, soups, quiches, and other assorted French-inspired items. It was located, along with the majority of other eateries, around the famous Galleria ice rink. They sat, ate, and watched the skaters wobble around the rink. Once she finished her meal, Lauren asked Declan if he would wait for her while she made a quick trip into a sporting goods store.

"Of course, please, go. I am quite entertained watching people go by and seeing a few of them over there"—he pointed to the rink—"fall flat on their butts."

When Lauren returned, Declan was no longer at the table. She turned and looked in every direction. Then she heard him call her name from the skate rental area just outside the rink.

"Come on," he said and gestured.

Lauren walked over to him. He was standing next to a bench wearing skates.

"I can't do that. I'll surely fall," she said, pointing to the extra pair of skates in Dec's hand.

"That'll make two of us," he said, giving her the skates. "I got you the same shoe size as my mom, since her sneakers seemed to fit you. But if they don't, you can get the right size over there."

"I think they'll be okay," she said. Declan stepped back and waited for her to put on the skates.

After one last firm swoop of the shoelace, Lauren stood. "I am ready for some serious bruising now."

Declan extended his hand, and they both wobbled onto the ice. Sporadically holding on to the rink walls and to each other, it took them thirty minutes and countless visits to the ice-cold surface before they finally completed one turn around the rink. It was a half hour in which they were constantly in contact—whether holding hands or falling on top of each other.

After dinner at Banti's Indian Cuisine, they went home and talked with Kate. She enjoyed hearing about their fun day, which, after their stint on the ice, had been followed by a visit to the Museum of Natural Science and the IMAX. They told Kate about some of the more amusing interactions and candid conversations they had. One of these interactions had culminated in Lauren throwing her new sports bra at Declan after he teased her about not telling him that she needed one that morning.

After a while, they went to their respective bedrooms and slept.

Laughter had been the common denominator of that amazing Sunday—the last day that Lauren thought of and addressed Declan as Dr. Baltierra.

TWENTY

"**G**ood morning, beautiful."

"Are you talking to me or the cat?" Kate asked as she dropped milk and strawberries into the blender.

"Both of you," Declan replied, his ongoing good mood a reflection of yesterday's pleasant outing with Lauren.

Blossom was sitting directly in front of his mother on the kitchen island, intrigued by the liquefying apparatus.

"Now, the question is, will she freak out when I turn it on?"

Declan gave his mother a kiss on the cheek. "We'll see. Is there enough in there for me?"

"Of course there is," she said.

"Where is Lauren?"

"She got up early this morning and said she wanted to go out and get herself an apartment. She also wanted to pick up a few personal things from someone she knew—that sort of thing."

"I could have taken her. How is she going to get around?"

"That's what I said. But she really seemed excited about doing these things herself, so I didn't push. It'd be a lot easier for her to get back on track if she had some of her documents with her. I'd love to put her on the payroll. We've been paying her cash for her work, and I think she feels weird about it."

"By the way, thanks again, Mom—about this whole thing."

"It's refreshing to have her around. And we really did need the help at the shop. On top of it all, I've completely fallen in love with this curious cat," Kate said while lightly petting Blossom's forehead.

The cat flinched when the blender ground to life, but remained in her place. She looked hypnotized by the twirling strawberry shake.

"I am paying her the same as everyone else. It should be enough for her to be independent." Kate stopped the blender and tapped on the lid. "So, what are you going to do today?"

"I'm gonna go run a few laps at Memorial Park, stop by the UT med library to pick up some articles I ordered, and then just bum around the rest of the day. Do you need me to do something?"

"Of course I do. There is always something for you to do around here," she said, "but after all these years, I've learned to manage. So, go ahead and be a bum."

—⁓ⱰⱰ—

Kate went to work, and Declan stuck to his plan for the day. Meanwhile, Lauren confronted a number of tribulations from the moment she set foot on the first of several buses that would take her around the city. The first hurdle came when she found herself without the correct bus fare. Embarrassed, she was forced to ask the long-faced, solemn, Monday morning crowd for help. A middle-aged man in the handicap section offered to break her ten-dollar bill. She thanked him and took a seat by the window. Belching a plume of black smoke down Fannin Street, the bus forged ahead along its route. People, cars, and buildings whizzed by in a blur as she stared out the window. Despite the setback with the bus fare, she looked outside with a growing sense of empowerment and optimism.

Lauren's most difficult task that day was not just to find her old friend Sandy but also to convince her that her life on the wrong side of the tracks was over. She was finally able to locate her at the downtown Starbucks where she worked.

"Oh my God!" Sandy exclaimed from behind the counter as soon as she saw Lauren. She murmured something to one of her fellow baristas and went around to meet her old friend with a hug. Both shed a few tears. Sandy grabbed Lauren by the arm and led her to one of the back tables. Once seated in front of each other, she took Lauren's hands and said in a stern yet friendly whisper, "You fucking bitch, where have you been all this time? I thought you were dead." Sandy wiped away a few more tears.

"I'm so, so sorry. You really can't possibly imagine how much, Sandy. In fact, I quite literally may have been dead," Lauren said.

"What do you mean?"

Except for a few interruptions where Sandy had to get up and make some lattes and mocha Frappuccinos, Lauren told her about her sobering hospital experience in Galveston.

"You are shitting me!"

"I wish I was shitting you. Trust me," Lauren told her, pulling her blouse down slightly and showing Sandy the top of her scar.

"Holy crap!" Sandy pressed her palms to her cheeks. "Lauren, this is insane. I can't believe it. I really don't think you are high and talking out of your ass because you look great, by the way. So, I have no option but to believe you. Honey, I feel so bad for you. But I am really glad you are here and alive."

"Thank you, Sandy."

"Well, what now?"

"Besides wanting to see you, I needed to find you so I could get my social security card and other documents I left at the apartment." Lauren paused, afraid to meet Sandy's eyes. "At *your* apartment, that is. I am sure you wouldn't want to live with me again, so I need that stuff to get my own place."

Sandy sighed. "Yeah, you really screwed me with the rent and all. But I survived. I still live in that shitty shoebox of a place. *Our* shitty shoebox, if you want to come back."

"Really?"

"Yes! You know I love you, and I am too damn lonely. Just promise—"

"Don't worry. No more hanging out with the wrong crowd. No more drugs or booze. No more insanity."

They sat for a while longer, talking about everything from Sandy's various jobs and her difficulties keeping up with college classes to Lauren's experiences since leaving the hospital. They also talked about everybody's new roommate, Blossom. Toward the end of their talk, they became excited when they realized that Lauren's new job would probably allow them to move to a better apartment complex. Sandy had to work until five, so Lauren's job was to go out and search for their new and hopefully improved home. They hugged each other again, and Lauren went on her way, sipping an iced coffee—on the house.

After getting ahold of her documents from the old apartment, Lauren set out to open a new bank account and then find a new apartment. She went to a variety of complexes, most located along US 59 and downtown. At some of the rental offices, she was immediately told that her lack of verifiable rental history would make her ineligible for a lease. Other apartment complexes were no more lenient. Still others were too expensive. She was disappointed. The area was likely to be the most convenient for her and Sandy, but while on a bus going west, she spotted a few apartment complexes just off the downtown area in an enclave known as Hedwig Village. The area seemed nice. She thought these would be too expensive but took a chance anyway and got off the bus. After a couple of additional rejections, she ran into a pleasant rentals associate at the Lakeview Apartments.

Lauren's luck changed when she got to Lakeview. The chatty older woman at the rental office shared a plethora of unsolicited life stories. Among other things, she got onto the subject of her carefree indulgence in fatty food and cigarettes, which led to the discovery of a common bond. Declan had performed open-heart surgery on them both.

"It's a small world, isn't it?" The sociable woman's forehead puckered as she leaned slightly over her desk toward Lauren. "Aren't you too young for heart disease?"

"I had a car accident. It was so bad that I had to get the blood vessels around my heart fixed."

"And you got lucky and got Dr. Baltierra. I was so lucky that my heart attack happened at the beach in Galveston because he fixed me up real good. Isn't he great? And so handsome too." She winked at Lauren.

"Yes, he is."

The expression on her face, though, said she was about to tell Lauren that she did not qualify for the lease. But first, the lady asked her, "Where did you say you worked?"

"As a matter of fact, I work at the Petal Inc., a flower retailer and distributor that happens to be owned by Dr. Baltierra and his mother."

The motherly woman looked at the papers in front of her for a second, sighed deeply, and turned them facedown on the desk. "Sweetie, I think that today I will bend the rules. This whole thing about 'approving' people can get a little silly. Besides, if you are remotely associated with that doctor, you must be all right. Let me do some new paperwork, and we will get you going."

"Are you sure? Thanks so much," Lauren said.

Lauren was told she could move into the new apartment in four weeks. She left the place feeling ecstatic. It was her first real, decent apartment. It had a pool and a tennis court. Above all, she was glad to have gotten it by herself—mostly. Unbeknownst to him, once again, Declan had helped her.

When Sandy finished up at work, she and Lauren both went to see their future home. They were as excited and hopeful as they had once been when they left their small hometown of Victoria a little over a year ago. They were able to sneak into the complex behind a resident who had just passed through the automatic gate. Both sat on a small bench next to the swimming pool, holding hands like the pair of high school best friends they had always been. The complex was a run-of-the-mill, lower-middle-class place not unlike countless others around the city, but to Lauren and Sandy, it was their entrance into a whole new world.

As it was beginning to get dark, Lauren said, "Sandy, I have to go."

"When do I get to meet all these nice people you've talked so much about?"

"Well, it's not that easy. I still feel a little shy around them, after all they've done for me. I mean, who does that?" Lauren hesitated. "So, it's a little odd right now."

"No problem. I totally understand."

"But I am sure sooner or later you will. You'll really like them."

They gave each other a hug and then took separate buses home.

—⁓—

Declan answered the door. "Hey, how did it go?"

Immediately, Blossom saw Lauren and went belly-up in the middle of the hallway.

"She missed you," he said.

"Yes, she did. She is just too spoiled, this one. Aren't you, Bloss?" Lauren said to the cat and picked her up. The three of them walked over to the library, where they joined Kate. "It went really well, by the way."

"We saved you some food—a little takeout from Whole Foods," Kate said.

"Oh, thank you, Mrs.—" Lauren paused and quickly rephrased. "Thank you, Kate. I will get some in a few minutes. I just wanted to let you know I found a place. And also, I found my friend Sandy. We talked, and we are going to share an apartment again. The new one will not be ready for a month, but I can move back in with her at our old place. If you want, I can move out as soon as tomorrow."

"Lauren, I don't want you to move out at all. I—" Kate glanced at Declan. "*We* just want to make sure you are safe and happy and ready to take on life again."

"Yes. Thank you so much," Lauren said. She tried to find the right way to express that she did not want to be a bother. Yet, while thinking about this, she came to the visceral realization that she never had been and never would be an inconvenience to them. She fully believed in their sincerity. Nonetheless, there was something that still made her feel slightly uncomfortable.

"I think my friend Sandy needs me as much as I need her. I would love to live in this beautiful place forever, but I think it's more…"

"Prudent?" Kate said, finishing Lauren's thought.

"That is a good word. It would be prudent for everybody, I guess," Lauren responded, still not satisfied with how she was expressing herself.

"Hey, we'll obviously see you at work and on occasion here at the house, right?" Kate asked. "Besides, I would like to have some sort of visitation rights for that little fur ball."

"Absolutely. No question about that," Lauren said. "I will let you get back to your reading. Would anyone like anything from the kitchen?"

"No, thank you," Kate answered, while Declan simply smiled and shook his head. As Lauren exited the room, she also gave Declan a brief glimmer of a smile.

Kate repositioned her glasses and went back to her book. Declan remained standing against the wall. He alternated looking at his mother and at the various bookshelves in the room. He remained as silent and as thoughtful as he had been throughout Lauren's narration of her day's events. In spite of this silence, there was a look of intense concentration on his face.

"I think the word is *emptiness*," Kate said without taking her eyes off the book.

He sighed. "That *is* a good word."

After a mutual exchange of kisses in the wind, Declan went to his room. From her deep leather couch, Kate lowered her book and looked at the spot where her son had just stood. She sighed too, feeling an instinctive and peculiar bit of maternal pain. She perceived an impending void in Declan, knowing that Lauren would be leaving soon.

TWENTY-ONE

I t is said that angels are, in a variety of ways, always watching over us.

When Lauren and Blossom were ready to move out of the house, Declan offered to give them a ride, but Lauren again declined.

"How will you take the cat on a bus?" he asked.

"I bought a pet carrier," Lauren said, "which is great, because everyone at the shop wants me to bring her with me every day."

"But…all your stuff. It can't be that easy to drag around all your belongings and a cat on public transportation."

"You forget, Dec. I have a single suitcase to my name."

"Right. Okay, I tried. I just wanted to make myself useful." Declan shrugged and tried to hide his disappointment.

"I know. I really appreciate that. You've done much more than enough. It's my turn to be useful and independent," Lauren said, meaning every word.

"Okay, then, I guess I will see you two at work."

—·—

Declan missed doctoring, but he truly enjoyed the opportunity to help people in situations far less grave than those of his usual clientele in Galveston. Over the next week, he woke up late and alternated jogging routines between Memorial Park and the nearby Rice University track. Afterward, he would go back home to clean up, pick up lunch for everyone at the shop, and then head over to distribute the food. Once there, he did all he could, from working the register to sweeping the floors. Everyone giggled and made it a point to ask Declan to clean this or that up. He always obliged. When it came to selling something to a new client, especially if the client happened to be a pretty female hotel rep, Declan was always asked to step up to the plate. These sales encounters involved a healthy amount of mutual flirting, which usually culminated in a decent business order for the shop. Yet none of these encounters resulted in a date. He was far from disappointed.

Some afternoons, Declan would hop in a van with whoever was delivering flowers. He took pleasure in personally delivering flowers, fruit baskets, balloons, and so on. He loved seeing where people lived or worked, and he enjoyed witnessing their reactions.

In spite of this pleasant routine, he felt a gap. His days fell just short of perfection. It was almost like not putting on that extra suture or surgical staple to make an incision look prettier, even if it wasn't technically needed. It was that last piece of a puzzle, which, although missing for the time being, was only temporarily misplaced. He had an idea of what it was and where to find it. But he hadn't put the puzzle together entirely by himself, and therefore, it would have been inappropriate for him to steal the satisfaction of fitting the last piece. Perhaps, he thought, last pieces are better left off. Perhaps the thrill of completing the puzzle, the elation that comes with a task achieved, the joy of passing the finish line, is transient and therefore anticlimactic.

Was Lauren the last piece of his puzzle? Perhaps. Perhaps.

Lauren's own puzzle was all but complete too, yet she felt certain the last piece was not hers to put into place. She had a good job and new friendships with normal, nice people. She felt that her only duty was to prove—mostly to herself—that putting the majority of the puzzle pieces together was in itself sufficient.

She excelled at this, and so she pushed away any emotion that diverged from a platonic friendship with Declan. Perhaps her goal was to make him proud of her, to let him know that his efforts had not been in vain. Perhaps he was just an instrument, an angel who had called on her to make something extraordinary out of the new life she'd been given. It wasn't her place to feel awkward when she saw him talking to those beautiful women in expensive suits buying thousands of dollars' worth of flowers. Perhaps that last puzzle piece was better left off.

Sometimes, if she didn't guard her thoughts, she found herself wondering, was Declan the last piece of her puzzle? Perhaps. Perhaps.

While not of the winged and haloed sort, a certain group of angels hinted to Declan and Lauren the possibility that the last piece of their respective puzzles might not only be one and the same but that it also deserved to be put in its place.

—⁂—

Angels Inc. was a Houston-based charity that helped children from Texas and Mexico with physical disabilities or who suffered from profound deafness. Their help ranged from the most basic support, such as providing clothing and recreational activities, to assisting in their medical care and procuring high-tech equipment such as electric wheelchairs. Kate Baltierra was one of their most active volunteers and financial supporters. On the third Sunday of Declan's month-long vacation, the organization had arranged for an outing at the zoo, to which Kate invited Declan and her employees, including Lauren.

Kate's group, along with dozens of other volunteers from the city, converged at the zoo's entrance around ten in the morning. Thirty or so kids arrived in vans. The volunteers organized themselves into groups and worked out all the logistics of providing lunch and dinner, as well as attending to the children's specific needs as they enjoyed the zoo. Declan knew sign language, so Kate asked him and Lauren to chaperone three children with congenital deafness. Two were eight-year-olds, Timmy and Roy, who had not responded to cochlear implants. The other boy was Maximiliano—Max for short—a nine-year-old with Waardenburg syndrome, a disorder that involves profound deafness, as well as deformities of the face, skull, and ears. They were otherwise normal kids.

Max had arrived in Houston from Mexico three months ago. The department of plastic surgery at the University of Texas Medical School at Houston, along with support from the Shriners Hospitals for Children and the Angels Inc. charity, had arranged for him to undergo two procedures that had now corrected a severe facial deformity. The last bandages had come off. Along with another group of children, he was simply waiting for one more child to finish her care at the other Shriners Hospital in Galveston before they could all be flown back home to Mexico—at no charge, thanks to Continental Airlines. Presently they were all staying at the Ronald McDonald House in the Texas Medical Center. Most had not seen their family for quite some time. Max wore an empty stare, and his facial expression seemed to be permanently locked in a frown.

Declan made the introductions.

"My name is D-e-c-l-a-n," he signed to the kids. "This is L-a-u-r-e-n."

Lauren waved hello to them. They returned the gesture with polite smiles—a somewhat protracted one from Max.

"Should we start from the beginning of the exhibits, or is there something you all are eager to see first?" Lauren asked. Declan translated.

"Elephants," Roy signed immediately. Timmy responded positively and excitedly at the suggestion.

"Elephants it is," Declan said and gestured so the kids would go on ahead of him and Lauren. The two Texan boys darted in front, while Max simply stood still. Lauren sensed his uneasiness and offered him her hand. He took it with one hand and instinctively offered the other one to Declan. The two grown-ups looked at each other with pleasant surprise. And magically, Max felt at ease. He smiled as they caught up with Timmy and Roy, who led them through the zoo's crowded pathways.

Three Asian elephants stood majestically, chewing on the mounds of hay scattered about them. Timmy, Roy, and eventually Max squeezed through the bodies in the crowd to finally end up pressed against the iron fence just outside the enclosure. They pointed and smiled, but the elephants seemed to nod at each other in apparent agreement to ignore the dozens of spectators.

Declan and Lauren observed from a short distance until the boys returned. This time they all held hands and walked toward the nearby white rhinoceros. There was a smaller number of people at this enclosure. It had an information plaque, but the boys essentially pulled Declan and Lauren everywhere with amazing energy, leaving them no time to take in the details.

Due to the typical Houston heat, it was all fun and giggles but with a lot of inevitable sweat. Declan realized that there was absolutely no way he could get through the big cats section without first getting some lunch and drinking a gallon or two of water.

"Okay, guys, it's time for lunch!" he said, signing to them simultaneously.

"Yeaheeeee," Timmy and Roy exclaimed. Max nodded happily.

"That sounds great. I am about to pass out," Lauren said, checking a map of the zoo. "There is a place just around the corner."

Whether by reading her lips or simply having a vague idea of what she was saying, Roy pulled her ahead by the hand. Despite his momentum, she extended her other hand just in time for the other two boys, and Declan at the end, to grab onto the human chain.

Declan paid for hamburgers, pizzas, hotdogs, chips, sodas, and water for everyone. Other kids and chaperones from their group were already at the concession stand. Most of the adults seemed just as tired and sweat drenched as Lauren and Declan.

Timmy and Roy found a group of pals at a shaded bench. Declan and Max joined them and began to unwrap their spoils. As she walked toward the kids with condiments in hand, Lauren observed the boys as they sat, eating and laughing. They were like any other children—the only difference was in how they communicated.

"These kids are amazing," she said to Dec, sitting down.

"Yes, they are. Hear that, Max?" He elbowed the boy lightly.

"Declan!" she said with a smile, but her eyes had a witty expression of disbelief.

"Oh, oops. You know what I mean," he said and immediately translated that to Max, who was now staring at him. The boy smiled with an air of comfort and reassurance. He told Lauren and Declan that he liked them very much, and then went back to his previous task of putting mustard on his hamburger. Lauren looked at the boy in admiration but with a hint of tears in her eyes.

A gentle breeze percolated through the shaded eating area. Although the air was warm, it felt surprisingly fresh. The three of them made small talk about the animals they had just seen. Lauren commented on the cuteness of the giraffes. Max agreed yet pointed out that they smelled terrible.

"Yes," Declan said, "it is a fact of the giraffe's life. I saw a program on National Geographic about that. I don't remember if it has to do with pheromones and mating or if it's some sort of defense mechanism." He realized Max probably wouldn't understand this, so he simply added in sign language, "Anyway, they are smelly but cute."

Max signed something back to Declan. Dec smirked and shook his head, which caused Max to look at Lauren and giggle.

"What?" she asked.

"Nothing."

"Come on, what did he say?"

"Nothing. It's boy-talk." Declan bobbed his head.

"Declan, come on. Am I going to have to hurt you two?" She pointed a water bottle at them.

"Okay, okay. He asked if I thought you were as cute as the giraffes."

"Oh," she said.

She leaned into the table and dipped a french fry in ketchup, a meditative expression on her face.

Declan was about to ask her if she was interested in what his answer had been, but a heavyset, middle-aged man approached their bench and sat next to Lauren. Declan recognized him as one of the administrators of Angels Inc. His safari outfit was drenched in sweat. He held a clipboard with a number of papers that were also bespattered with perspiration.

"It is my understanding that Kate's boy is a handsome chap," he said, his words honed by a British accent. "Aside from the children, you two are the most beautiful people here, so I figured you must belong to our organization's Irish darling."

"Indeed, she is my mother," Declan told him.

"Splendid," he said, fanning himself with his hat. "I'm Bob, formerly Robert from London. I thought I would come and make your acquaintance, as I will surely need a heart transplant after these kids are through with me today."

"I think we all will," Lauren said.

"You must be Kate's lovely guest, Lauren." He gave her a nervous smile and turned his attention back to Declan. In a lower voice, he said, "I wanted to pose a rather sensitive suggestion, if you might entertain it."

Declan didn't know where Bob was headed, but he didn't really have a choice except to hear him out. "Sure, shoot."

Bob looked at the sky as if in search for the right words. He cleared his throat. "So, you have met my good friend Max here.

He is a fantastic young man who has been through quite a whirl-wind. I will spare you most of the details, but as it turns out, he is not due back to his family for two more weeks—on the group flight with the rest of the kids. The problem is, his mother has called about having him return by the end of the week so he may take part in First Communion exercises next Saturday along with his sister and cousins. This is so important to them that they have offered to send me money that I am certain they can't really spare, to have him back in time."

Declan still didn't have a notion about where Bob was going with this.

"In addition, there is another child whom we expect to fin-ish his treatment soon. He could surely use a seat on the group flight—the seat that Max would free up if he returned to Mexico this week. Do you dig where I am coming from, my dear doctor?"

"Not quite," Declan said.

"Indeed. I'll be frank, then. I am asking if there is a chance you would want to accompany Max back to Mexico this week, deliver him to his family, and thus free up a seat on the group flight for the other boy two weeks hence. Of course, while you foot the bill for the entire excursion. How is that for frankness?"

"That's pretty good. I appreciate it." Declan thoughtfully absorbed the words of this somewhat comical-looking but ded-icated person.

"In case you are wondering," Bob continued, "Kate did men-tion to me that you are on vacation and that you don't miss a chance to spend time in Mexico. I do occasionally observe the difference between being frank and being inordinately imposing, you know. Besides, it seems like it would be a good occasion for you and your girlfriend here to take a boat ride on Chapultepec Lake."

Lauren and Declan glanced at each other quickly and broke into a faint laugh.

Bob realized his mistake and said, "Oh, I am quite sorry, I thought…"

"No worries," Declan said. "Going back to your request, I think it sounds feasible."

"Fantastic! I took the liberty of researching fares, here." He handed Declan a sheet of paper with several flights from an internet search.

Dec glanced at the column of flights. "This one on Tuesday afternoon seems like a winner."

"Max here will be waiting for you at the Ronald McDonald House. I will have it all arranged," Bob said graciously. "You are most certainly your mother's progeny. A doctor and a gentleman." He worked his way off the bench. "Now I have to go on to other 'requests.' Please let Max know. He will be very happy about this. Cheers!" he said before walking away to another table.

"Go figure!" Declan exclaimed, looking at Lauren.

"Are you going to tell Max now?"

"No, I will tell him when we are done with today's outing," he said, patting the boy's shoulder.

Max looked at them with an ample grin that sported a drop of ketchup. He was unaware of the exact nature of the adult conversation that had just transpired.

Everyone gathered outside the zoo in the evening. The vans had already pulled up to the curb, and Bob Worthington was taking a head count. Volunteers helped to manage this last step, bone-tired and ready to go home.

The Ronald McDonald House shuttle was the last to arrive. As the children got on the bus, Declan took Max aside and, in sign language, made him aware of the plan for Tuesday. Max yelped with joy and threw himself with open arms at Declan. Then he ran to Lauren and hugged her around the waist. Max made a number of quick signs to her.

Declan translated, "Do you want to go to Mexico?"

"Huh?" Her eyebrows rose.

"Well, Max wants us both to go and be his Communion godparents. It's like being second-string godparents. In Mexican culture, basically, you get a godparent—more like a sponsor—for every major event in your life."

"Oh, wow, I don't think so," she said, still looking puzzled. "I mean, that's great, but you know, it's probably something really important for him and his family and…I don't think I'd be able to go."

"Yeah, it sounds crazy. Besides, his parents surely already have real godparents lined up for him," Declan said.

Declan squatted down again in front of Max, and they became engrossed in a sign language conversation. After the apparent linguistic bartering seemed to reach an end, the two shook hands and Max marched toward Lauren. He grabbed her hand, pulled her into a quick stoop toward him, and placed a kiss on her cheek. Then he ran to the van. Once the van started to pull away, they exchanged goodbye waves with Max through the window.

"What was all that about?" Lauren asked.

"It's funny. We just went back and forth about whether he could have more than one Communion godfather. He pointed out that he has lots of godfathers for other things and that I could be like them. I told him that for this particular event, his parents probably have one already selected. Anyway, after a bit more negotiation, he was satisfied."

"Just like that?" she asked.

"Well, sort of. He said that if I couldn't be his godfather, then he'd really want the both of us to go and see him through Communion. He has memorized his catechism, you know."

"And what did you tell him?"

Declan scratched his head, a guilty smile on his face. "I told him okay."

Lauren was concerned about missing work at the shop, about not having a passport, and about the fact she could not afford to purchase a plane ticket. Declan drove her back to her apartment. During the ride, he assured her that Kate would love for her to get away for a while and see a different environment. "Besides," he told her, "it's for a good cause." He also informed her that she could get a passport expedited in a day at the downtown passport office. Finally, with regard to the plane ticket and expenses, he simply said, "Don't be silly."

When they walked into Lauren's tiny apartment, Sandy was home.

"So, you are Dr. Dec, huh?" Sandy asked.

"In the flesh," he responded.

After the introductions, he accepted Sandy's invitation to stay for a cup of coffee. The three of them sat around a makeshift coffee table made up of a message corkboard on top of a pink plastic milk crate. There was only one chair, which Blossom had claimed, relegating the humans to the carpet.

"We are still working on the furniture," Lauren said.

"It's gonna be delivered to our new apartment directly from Italy, you know," Sandy joked.

"Only the best for the cat, I see," Declan said.

Declan and Lauren went over all the events that had led to the unexpected trip to Mexico. Sandy wanted to know where they would stay and whether they were going to share a room. Lauren's cheeks turned cherry red.

"No need to panic. I totally took this for granted and failed miserably at putting you at ease," Declan said, turning to Lauren. "We will shack up with my uncle David. He lives in a huge condo in the heart of the city. My two cousins have families of their own now. One lives in Paris and the other one in Monterrey. They left behind a large, comfortable empty nest with plenty of bedrooms to go around. So, now that we are all settled," he said, getting up off the carpet and pulling Blossom into his arms for a goodbye hug, "I think I should go home to get the tickets before the flight runs out of seats." He ruffled Blossom's fur. "By the way, how will this monkey fare in your absence?"

"Don't worry, I'll take care of her," Sandy said.

"Well, I was wondering if it would be okay if my mother took her in for a few days. She really misses her," Declan said. "Besides, you two will have her forever after."

Lauren and Sandy nodded in agreement.

"Okay, ladies, we'll call it a night." Declan set down Blossom, who quickly reclaimed her throne on the chair. Then he looked at Lauren. "I'll pick you up at seven so we can be first in line at the passport office."

They turned in her application by nine a.m. on Monday, and Lauren's passport would be ready by four. Before they returned to pick it up, they went shopping. Declan got gifts for his aunt and uncle, and for a couple of other people. He also gave Lauren a ride to work, taking Blossom along, so that Kate would take the kitty home at the end of the workday.

"Did you tell Lauren that you plan to stay until Sunday and what to pack?" Kate asked her son that evening

"I told her that I was only going to take a pair of jeans and a handful of shirts."

"Brilliant!" Kate said sarcastically and promptly called Lauren to give her better instructions.

A few minutes later, when Kate came into the TV room, Declan was slouched on the couch with Blossom on his chest. He was watching *Extreme Makeover*.

"I love this show," she said.

"Really?" Declan asked, surprised.

"I watch it all the time. It's amazing. Some of the transformations these people undergo are pretty incredible."

"I was this close to being a plastic surgeon, you know?"

"I know. And you would have been a great one too. But you know what? Lauren—and this little one, for that matter—might not have entered our lives had you made that choice." She squeezed his forearm. He nodded knowingly but quickly turned his attention to the TV.

They watched the show until Declan started to get a little too technical in his observations, and Kate decided it was time for bed. She gave him a kiss and proceeded upstairs.

"Mom?"

"Yes?" He heard her pause midway up the staircase.

"Thank you," he said.

"Have a great time and take care of her."

"I will," Declan said with a smile. He felt excited about the prospect of tomorrow and the next few days.

—⁂—

Max gave Declan a hug soon after he entered the living room at the Ronald McDonald House. A slender and elegant older woman stood next to Max's kid-sized roller suitcase. Once Dec straightened, she introduced herself and they had a brief, cordial chat. She then inspected Declan's ID and gave him a few papers to sign and to take with him.

"We are going to miss you, buddy," she said to Max.

Declan was not sure what the boy had understood, but Max immediately replied in a barrage of hand signals.

"He said, 'Me too,' in case you are wondering," Declan told her.

"Oh, come here," the lady said and gave Max a hug. "Now, go away before I ruin my makeup."

Declan grabbed the luggage with one hand and held Max's hand with the other.

"Have a good trip, Dr. Baltierra," she said just before the door closed behind them.

Max's overall expression was kind of sad once they were in the car. He did not sign anything for a few miles and simply looked out the window as if in a trance. At a stop sign before getting on the 610 Loop, Declan finally figured it out. While he was sure the boy would be sad to leave Houston and the few friends he had made, his gloomy state was something else.

Just before the light turned green, Declan signed, "We are on our way to pick her up right now." Out of the corner of his eye, he detected an almost magical transformation of the boy's face. They continued in a happy silence until they arrived at Lauren's apartment. They saw her sitting on her front stoop. As soon as Declan parked the car, Max flew out the door. He gave Lauren a hug and then grabbed her duffel with one hand and her hand with the other. He pulled her toward the car. Declan got out and helped put the luggage in the trunk.

"I'll sit in the back—you boys can be pilot and copilot on our way to the airport," Lauren said.

Declan translated and then gave them both a thumbs-up.

They had close to an hour to kill before boarding, so Declan suggested they find a place to have lunch. He and Lauren gave Max the choice, on account of it being his last day in Houston. When he chose McDonald's, Declan asked him if he was absolutely sure, since he could certainly eat at one in Mexico.

"Yes," Max signed back, and added, "because my family doesn't go to McDonald's."

Declan understood. "Mickey D's it is."

All the tables at the food court were taken. Lauren suggested they go to the gate and eat there. So, they sat on a row of seats looking out at the Continental jetliner. Declan and Max exchanged myriad signs in between eating and pointing at different things on the airplane. Midway through the meal, the ketchup ran out. Lauren volunteered to go get more, but Declan insisted he would go get it.

Declan was on his way back, armed with a handful of Heinz Ketchup packets and extra napkins, when suddenly he stopped just across from the gate where Lauren and Max sat. As he stood there, a motorized cart full of passengers whizzed by and startled him. In one of those eternal yet frozen seconds in time, he experienced a glimpse of something he was not sure how to interpret. He felt like a tree trying to look across the highway through the occupants of a passing car, wondering what it would be like to live on the other side. Would the ground and the wind and the water and the life be different over there? Better? Worse? Would it be safe and worthwhile to try that side? How could it be done? With these questions bouncing around in his head, he looked at Max and the radiant Lauren. He thought about his friends from college and even medical school who often talked about their DVD-equipped minivans or showed him pictures from their wallets exhibiting everyone in their family, including their pets. *Could that ever be me?* he had asked himself, not particularly searching for an answer. *I guess it could,* said a voice from an unknown corner of his mind. In fact, he instantly realized that in the eyes of most people who surrounded them at the gate, the three of them were the spitting image of a young, blissful family.

Declan shook his head and came back from that glimpse into a hypothetical life. He resumed his step and delivered the ketchup to Lauren and Max.

Once they were in line for the jetway, and holding Max's hand, Lauren casually whispered to Declan that she had never flown before.

"Oh," he replied. "Don't worry, if need be, we'll coach you through it."

"Thanks," she said.

On the plane, Declan secured their luggage in the overhead compartment. Max asked for the window, so they let him go first. Lauren followed into the middle seat, and Declan took the aisle.

As the plane taxied, Declan could feel Lauren's apprehension. It was not until the engines erupted in a loud roar and their bodies were pressed against the seats as the plane accelerated down the runway that Declan felt an odd jealousy. He was envious of the armrests flanking Lauren, to which she held on for dear life. Oh, how he suddenly wanted to take, and could have taken, her hand. But all he could muster were several minutes of silence.

Finally, he said, "Hey, this is the worst of it. It should get better from now on."

She nodded with her eyes closed. Declan and Max looked at each other and smiled. Declan mentally hit himself on the forehead: *Yeah! Way to coach her through this, man.* In truth, he was unsure how much reassurance or support to show Lauren without smothering her. In the past, when presented with this kind of scenario with the opposite sex, it had never been so difficult for him to assess a situation and feel that he was acting appropriately. This was true in all of his past relationships. Seldom had he found himself in the uncomfortable position of not knowing how to act or react in front of women. Why the trouble now?

Once the plane leveled off, Lauren's anxiety eased. She opened her eyes.

Max signed to Declan that he would share his window seat if they wanted to look out. Declan told him not to worry, and he also used that opportunity to tell Lauren a few things, pretending it was coming from Max.

"Max wants me to tell you not to be afraid. He has flown a few times back and forth and says that it has always been okay. He also wanted me to mention that there is occasional turbulence, which feels kind of like a bumpy road, but that it's also okay. And if you feel really sick, there are little baggies in that seat pocket." He gave her a silly grin.

She smiled back and said, "Thanks, so far so good."

After a couple of hours, the bit of advice regarding turbulence came in handy on the plane's approach to Mexico City.

The descent into the city was almost always bumpy. Perhaps it was due to air currents created by the mountains that encircled the metropolis. Some people, of the more cynical sort, blamed the turbulence on the city's pervasive smog. Others, maybe of a more spiritual persuasion, argued it was an act of warning created by the snow-covered Popocatépetl volcano to the east; it eternally guarded the Valley of Mexico and the spirit of its beloved Iztaccíhuatl—an adjacent volcano, whose peaks resembled the silhouette of a sleeping woman.

Every man, woman, and child of the city knew the legend of the volcanoes, which were once human and deeply in love. The myth said that before Popocatépetl, a fierce warrior, could marry his lover, he had to prove his worth and defeat an army in a faraway land. While he achieved victory, false information got back to Iztaccíhuatl before he could return home. She was told that her lover had died in battle, and she perished of a broken heart. When Popocatépetl returned and found Iztaccíhuatl, he carried her body to a secluded spot deep in the valley. Once there, he couldn't bear to bury his lover and not ever see her again. Kneeling next to her, his sorrow proved too great. He also perished of grief. From a distance, the Aztec gods took note of their mutual, indomitable love and benevolently turned them into mountains so that they could spend eternity, alive, at each other's side. And it is thus that Popocatépetl, a live volcano that frequently gushes smoke from its top, warns newcomers approaching his and his eternal lover's domain.

—⁘—

The immigration and customs lines were endless. Two jumbo jets had arrived from Europe almost simultaneously, just a few minutes before their own flight. Nearly an hour later, they presented all their necessary immigration documents to the agent, who carefully reviewed the notarized letter that Max's parents had faxed ahead of time to give permission for the boy to travel with Declan.

They finally cleared customs. Just out of the sliding exit doors, they found themselves in front of a sea of people waiting for hundreds of other passengers. Declan decided that the best way to find Max's family was to display the boy atop his shoulders. Not too long after he did this, a girl not much older than Max tugged at Declan's shirt. In Spanish, she said, "Hello, mister, we are over there." She pointed toward Max's parents, who found it difficult to contain tears of joy upon seeing their boy back at last. Declan put Max down and the boy ran to his family.

Declan and Lauren stood not too far behind the hugs and kisses that continued to multiply as numerous other relatives began to materialize from among the surrounding crowd. They all examined the boy's face in joyous disbelief. He was now a normal, rather handsome kid. Some of the family members gave thanks to God, others to the Virgin Mary, and others to the Virgin of Guadalupe for what they felt was a miracle. Eventually, Max's father locked eyes with Declan and extended his hand as he walked toward him. Dec introduced himself and then Lauren. The man also gently shook her hand. By this time, Max's mother and several other family members had lined up to shake Declan's and Lauren's hands and bestow hugs. It was almost as if they thought that the two of them were directly responsible for Max's transformation. They'd become the emblem for all the volunteers, from financial donors to doctors to administrators to van drivers et cetera, who had actually made this day and the boy's new future possible.

Once the initial emotions receded, Declan asked the boy's father to seal Max's journey by signing the last release document. As soon as this was done, the man collected an envelope from his wife and offered it to Declan. It was a simple but meticulous invitation to Max's and his sister's First Communion event, written in calligraphy. The man also told him it would be an honor to have the two of them stay in their home as guests. In the most polished and courteous Spanish, Declan told him they'd be delighted to attend the celebration. He also explained that he was grateful for his kind offer but that their lodging was already arranged.

The man gave them one more handshake and a hug before letting them get their luggage. They said goodbye to all, including Max, who had been standing next to Lauren for a while now. Soon, Declan and Lauren found themselves alone, in a money exchange booth.

"Ready?" he asked Lauren, folding the peso notes into his wallet.

"Wow. I am overwhelmed. But yes, I am all yours," Lauren said with an animated smile, followed instantly by a sudden blush. "I mean, I am totally clueless about what to do or where to go, so, yes, lead the way."

The way was a walk down the long main airport hallway that eventually came to a subway station. Declan bought tickets, and they boarded a train. During the ride, he told Lauren that his uncle David had offered to pick them up at the airport but that Declan loved taking public transportation. He knew the city like the back of his hand. They made a subway line transfer and soon got off at the Auditorio station.

Right off the train was a long, wide corridor decorated with pieces of art and cultural artifacts. A steep set of stairs brought Declan and Lauren to a lush area on Chapultepec Avenue. This avenue ran along a colossal park where people were enjoying the pleasant weather. Some parkgoers sat on benches, some walked their dogs, some played, others slept, and many others appeared to be working—selling everything from food to shoeshines. Declan pointed out the imposing National Auditorium on the other side of the street. He told Lauren that, while there were countless theaters in the city, this place was the main venue for world-class concerts and productions. As they continued to walk, Dec pointed to a row of luxury skyscraper hotels behind which, he said, lay the residential enclave named Polanco. He had grown up there, and it was as good as home. They walked through the lobby of the Hotel Nikko and exited onto the streets of a beautiful neighborhood with tall green trees and colorful flowers. The homes seemed to be squeezed tightly and monotonously next to one another. Closer inspection invariably revealed the sophisticated façades of some of Mexico City's mansions. Lauren peeked through a few of the homes' gates. She saw sprawling, manicured lawns in front of houses that ranged in style from art deco to ultramodern.

After walking several more blocks, they stopped in front of a black gate at 24 Melville. Declan studied the gate and remarked, "Huh, they changed the door on me."

"Is this your uncle's house?"

"Nope. Here, take a look." He lifted the mail slot on the gate.

"Holy shhh—!" Lauren exclaimed, curtailing the second word. She was astonished to see a much larger version but almost an exact replica of Kate's Spanish-style home in Houston. "Let me guess, this is where you grew up?"

"Indeed it is. Unfortunately, it seems the new owners put up this nasty gate, and I see they've made other changes. But oh well, it's their house now." Declan shrugged. "Across the street lives a couple who are one of my family's best friends. We are running the risk of having them spot us if we stay here much longer. They would then trap us and force us to visit for the rest of the week. So, let's move on."

They proceeded north a few more blocks and then turned left on Presidente Masaryk Avenue. This was the commercial heart of the neighborhood. Chic outdoor cafés, high-end retailers, and the finest automobiles flanked the avenue.

"Have you always been rich?" Lauren asked.

"Well..." He thought for a second. "I've never lacked anything substantial."

"You always know what to say," she observed. Then, while stopping in front of a swanky necklace behind the thick window at the Cartier store, Lauren added, "But you are not just 'doctor rich.'"

"What do you mean?"

"I mean, most people think of doctors as having lots of money. Which I guess you have."

"Actually, I get paid very little at UTMB. I am still a fellow," he interrupted. "But you are correct. I am well-off, mostly through my mother's business and my father's bequests."

"I know. Yet your family and your origins here kinda go beyond that. Your and Kate's wealth is more of culture, of being good to people, of being educated…It's as established as this neighborhood. You are rich in a different way. A good way." She bobbed her head thoughtfully. "Maybe I'm wrong, but you strike me as someone who could buy this," she said, and pointed at the necklace in the window, "but won't because it's really gaudy. I mean, I don't know. Anyway, I don't know what I am talking about." Lauren was flustered.

"We have means, but we are humble. Maybe that's what you mean. It's what my mom and dad taught me, particularly growing up in this city full of contrasts. I've always kept in mind that not too far from here, the view is completely different. Beyond what you see around here, you'll find people whose lives range from middle class to indigent. But that's the Mexico I've always known. I've tried to rationalize, accept, and understand the differences among all kinds of people. And I respect them all the same."

"Again, Dec, you found the right thing to say," she told him.

"Okay, subject change. That, over there, is our target." He pointed down the street to a beautiful, seven-story, white condominium building framed by silver windows, their ledges replete with lush flowers.

"How nice!" Lauren walked alongside Declan as they made their way to the building. They entered the lobby and were greeted by Don Manuel, a sixtyish, chubby doorman in an impeccable uniform, who instantly recognized Dr. Declan and referred to him as such.

"I am so pleased to see you again. I wish you could visit us more. This must be the charming companion Mrs. Tere said you would bring. I have known this one since he was this big," he said to a language-bewildered Lauren, indicating with his finger the approximate height of Declan as a child. Not understanding Spanish, she simply smiled and nodded but Declan promptly translated. "Please, please, come on in," Don Manuel said, ushering them toward the elevator.

Before getting through the doors, Declan unzipped his backpack and produced a box of Macallan Scotch and offered it to the appreciative gentleman.

"You shouldn't have."

"I know," Declan told him, now with his back toward the deep end of the elevator. "I wanted to. See you later, Don Manuel."

The doors closed.

The ride up to the penthouse took only a few seconds. This allowed the jolly doorman downstairs to call up and announce their arrival.

As soon as the door opened, a Revlon-blond, svelte, and elegant woman in her late fifties stood before them with open arms and maybe just a touch of superfluous jewelry. She first hugged Lauren. She proceeded with the traditional Latin custom of delivering a kiss on the cheek, which caught Lauren off guard. In a synchronized move, she placed the same quick kiss on Declan, put her arm through one of Lauren's, and in heavily accented but perfect English, told her that she was glad to welcome her into their family. She led her into the house. Declan was essentially ignored in all this. He just smiled at his aunt's over-the-top personality.

With his and Lauren's luggage in hand, Declan followed them through a skylighted anteroom that led to the living room. The décor was antique European accented by Mexican paintings and sculptures from the classic midcentury masters, Kahlo, Rivera, and Tamayo. Other pieces were glasswork and nondescript statutes made of obsidian. While Teresa gave Lauren a tour of her approximately five-thousand-square-foot abode, Declan homed in on the fantastic smells emanating from the kitchen.

As quickly as he could, he slid his bag into the former room of his cousin Eduardo. Then he headed to the main guestroom at the back of the penthouse and placed Lauren's duffel on the bed. Promptly, he dashed to the kitchen and found two middle-aged ladies preparing a meal. He did not know them. His aunt's longtime housekeeper-cook-confidant had recently passed away. Nonetheless, he introduced himself and warned them that he could not help his famished state and that he would help himself to a sandwich. They smiled, and one of them handed him a plate with sliced French bread. On it, Declan slapped a couple of ham and cheese slices he'd snagged from the fridge.

After eating, he grabbed some water and joined Lauren and Teresa. They were only halfway through the tour and presently in the library that overlooked a central courtyard. As soon as Tere saw the two bottles of mineral water in Dec's hand, she exclaimed to Lauren, "Oh, my dear, I am terribly sorry. I whisked you away without offering you anything to drink. This is quite unlike me. I am just so excited to have you here." She looked at Declan and said, "I'm glad to have you here too, Dec."

"Thanks," he said.

"Let's finish up showing you *your* house, Lauren. Then we can sit for an early dinner. We are going to have sesame scallops and red snapper in a tamarind sauce."

Lauren looked surprisingly at ease. "That sounds incredible. I can't wait."

"Neither can I," Declan said.

"I bet you can't. Don't think I didn't notice a little extra noise in the kitchen," his aunt said in Spanish. Then, back in English, she said to Lauren, "This one has always been a bit of a glutton. I swear, I don't know why he's not as big as an elephant." They both giggled.

They eventually ended up in Lauren's room, where Tere said, "You will find just about everything you need here, from towels in the bathroom to blankets in that armoire. There is a minibar over there. I become suspicious if it isn't used on a regular basis. Now, Declan, let's give her some time alone to freshen up." Teresa put her arm through Declan's and walked away.

Once they were out of the room, he explained why it would be best if they laid low on the subject of alcohol. In a whisper, his aunt exclaimed, "Dear Jesus, that's right! Kate told me all about it. I don't know what I was thinking. Anyway, I do have a lot of different options, minus alcohol."

"Aunt Tere, I think if you offer her one of your great concoctions and have to make the point that it's nonalcoholic, it might make her feel bad."

Teresa put the back of her hand to her forehead and rolled her eyes, recognizing he had an excellent point. "I am sorry to be a little off. I'm just unusually excited about you two being here. Anyway, go freshen up. I will see you at the dinner table."

"Thank you," he said and went to his room.

—⁂—

As Lauren freshened up, she had time to reflect on all the recent activity in her life. Not too long ago, her introduction to Kate had felt surreal. But this whole new experience in Mexico went way beyond her wildest dreams. How could complete strangers, from a whole different country no less, make her feel so much like family?

She walked over and opened the french doors in her room. These led to a private sunroom. The far wall was made of river rocks and had a triple-level fountain. The translucent roof had a gap between the walls along their perimeter, which explained the two birds bathing in the top part of the fountain and not minding Lauren's presence. The other walls were covered with vines, bougainvillea, and evenly spaced pots of other flowers. Two cherrywood lounges were in the middle of the space, on each side of a short, matching table. Lauren took a deep breath and, while slowly exhaling, walked back into the bedroom.

She stood in front of the bathroom sink and looked at her unmade face in the mirror. With her thumbs and index fingers, she rubbed her ears and felt the lingering tiny cavities left over by a number of former earrings. Her cheeks felt smooth, yet she thought there was a certain uneven contour to the undersurface of her eyes. She wondered if she was or if she could ever be pretty. Would she ever wear the right makeup? What did Teresa Baltierra, a woman with such imposing presence, think of her unadorned exterior? What did Declan think? Lauren pulled away from the mirror, shut her eyes, and concentrated on a sudden, embalming silence that was broken only by the two squabbling birds around the fountain.

Exhaling out of her momentary trance, she hastily washed and dried her face. She took a small, square, plastic cosmetics bag from her suitcase. From this, she removed and applied deodorant. With a brush and a rubber hair band, Lauren went back to the mirror. She brushed her hair and adjusted it into a simple ponytail. Then she changed her top for a similar one in a different color. Just as she stared at the bottom of her sparse cosmetics bag, where she saw a lousy set of mascara, blush, eyeliner, and a golden, chipped tube of lipstick, someone knocked at the door.

She opened it to find Declan. He had rescued her again from dwelling on her perceived inadequacies. Unbeknownst to her, one thing was certain: Lauren Madison was unequivocally beautiful.

TWENTY-TWO

"It seems Rif wants to go out for his nightly walk, honey," I told Frank.

"How about we just let him out back. I don't want you to lose your train of thought."

"Fine, but go out and give him a little attention. In the meantime, I will pick up around here. We'll continue the story upstairs."

"Sounds good," Frank said.

A short while later, I continued relating what I knew about Declan and Lauren's experience on that trip to Mexico.

Declan's uncle David was the oldest sibling of the three brothers that included Declan's father. He was the director of the National Medical Center. He had faculty appointments at the five medical schools in the city and hospital privileges at most of the major hospitals of the country. His professional curriculum vitae was about an inch thick, which included abstracts from dozens of articles he had published in major medical journals and overviews of his two texts on gastroenterology.

Despite a busy day at work, David had been able to join them. He did not want to miss dinner on the first day of his beloved nephew's visit. And he was eager to meet Lauren, whom he liked instantly. Toward the end of a delectable meal filled with congenial conversation, David suggested that rather than having dessert at home, Declan should take Lauren to one of the many nearby cafés.

"I will not see you again tonight or tomorrow morning. You must enjoy your stay with us and fall in love with this frenzied but engaging city," he told Lauren as he helped her ease into a sweater while standing in the foyer. "And, Dec, do come by the office tomorrow. I was able to get ahold of Beto, who would love to see you and Lauren for lunch. Let's say, twelve thirty?"

"I look forward to that," Declan replied, glad his uncle had made the suggestion. Also, he was happy he'd be able to see his old friend from college the next day.

Lauren and Declan disappeared behind the elevator doors as the older couple waved goodbye with subdued excitement, just like parents sending their child off on a first date. What David and Teresa probably had in mind at the time became apparent to Dec and Lauren on the quiet elevator ride down. Surprisingly, they did not feel uncomfortable at all.

Declan offered Lauren his arm. With their elbows interlocked, the couple stepped out into the crisp but agreeable evening air as Don Manuel affably held open the door for them. They walked almost in unison through the now quiet and dimly lit street. Soon they reached the more boisterous, brilliantly illuminated commercial street nearby. Declan and Lauren heard but did not listen to the sounds of cars going by, the bewildering voices of the multitudes sitting outside cafés and restaurants, or the muffled music emanating from a small boom box tucked behind a valet parking podium. They breathed in but did not smell the now slightly cleaner air of a city that desperately does its best to purify itself nightly from the literal exhaust of daytime life.

Declan decided on El Moro, a café known for doling out the best churros and hot chocolate since 1935. They shared but did not quite fully taste the establishment's otherwise phenomenal offerings. They left the café and continued to explore the area.

A vague but almost electrifying feeling of happiness and repose was all they knew as their elbows touched while walking or when they hastily crossed the busy Masaryk and Homero Avenues with a firm grip on each other's hand. Their conversation was nothing more than small talk, sustained by the pleasure of mutual contact. They felt content to ignore the events that had drawn them together. Their state of mind made it easy to walk back to the house just before midnight and not feel one ounce of awkwardness when they bid each other good-night.

They withdrew to their respective bedrooms and slept peacefully. There was no uncertainty or curious excitement or nervousness. It was as if they had just been given the gift of perspective, which made them realize that their friendship and affection had irreversibly evolved.

Fate not only determined that evolution but also arranged for the moment that would forever mark the transition of their relationship. This happened on the following day at the Tacubaya subway station.

Teresa Baltierra felt that eight o'clock in the morning was a good time to knock on their doors, inquire if they had slept well, and advise them that breakfast would be served shortly.

"Good morning, Mrs. Baltierra," Lauren said as she walked into the kitchen.

"Good morning, Lauren. I hope you didn't mind me waking you two up. I just thought that since you are having lunch close to noon, it would be best to have an early breakfast. Besides, knowing Declan, he would have slept all day. It's a well-known fact of the Baltierra clan. Please, dear, grab that basket. We are all set up on the terrace. Come."

Teresa took ahold of a carafe of pomegranate juice and led Lauren through the main living room to a spacious balcony overlooking the street below. Its floor was made of concrete, beautifully painted in blue-green tones intended to mimic a walk through the ocean. A chromed metal spiral staircase led to the roof.

Lauren followed Teresa up the stairs and encountered what was nothing short of a small park. Plots of manicured grass and walkways lined with flowers and metal benches all converged at a central space with a picnic table shaded by large patio umbrellas. A waist-high concrete fence covered in ivy enclosed the rooftop garden. Even through the haze of smog beyond the confines of the cityscape, Lauren could discern the distant outlines of mountains.

"Your garden is as beautiful as ever, Aunt Tere," Declan said as he walked up behind them. He gave his aunt a quick kiss on the cheek. "Lauren, how did you sleep?"

"Very well, thank you," she answered.

"This looks amazing," he said, pointing to an attractive spread of juices, cereal, and fruit. He lifted the lid off a couple of serving bowls containing scrambled eggs, bacon, and beans.

"Well, enjoy," Teresa said, and the three of them sat and ate over light conversation about how the roof garden had come to fruition over the years.

The subway system in Mexico was known simply as El Metro. It was the product of a city that found itself in an abrupt transition into modernity and with a dire need to mobilize a population that nearly doubled in the decade following the Second World War. The former lands of the Aztecs were sacrificed to gargantuan machines, given up to metal, concrete, and sweat to produce the first subway line in 1969. Mexico City joined a handful of other cities around the world in providing its dwellers fast, accessible, and cheap transportation. Over the next three decades, the subway system grew to twelve lines that transported nearly five million people daily.

An escalator carried Lauren and Declan to the abyss of the Polanco metro station. They went directly to a glass-shielded booth, behind which an attendant yawned in excruciating boredom before eventually handing Declan a packet of tickets and a few coins in change. They each slid a ticket through the automated turnstiles. Only a few people were waiting on the platforms, most of whom seemed to be working class and employed in that privileged sector of town.

An air current rushed from the tunnel just before an orange train emerged. They boarded and stayed on until the line's second-to-last station, Tacubaya, a transfer point to Line 9—which would then take them to the National Medical Center. As soon as they entered the main hub of the station, Lauren gasped at the dramatic change of atmosphere. The modest crowds of the previous subway stations had now turned into a swarm. Countless people walked and ran every which way through the massive hub. The hallways were a mall of businesses. Thunderous noises, conversations, music of every genre, the distinctive voice of a man hawking lottery tickets—it all seemed like pandemonium to Lauren. Declan, however, was in his element. Like every person there, he knew that everything around them was normal. The apparent bedlam had order to it and was, in the end, quite uncomplicated. In spite of this, prudence instinctively set in, and he swiftly grasped Lauren's hand as they both dove into the current of people flowing toward the boarding platforms of Line 9. They arrived at the next ramp and waited only a short time for the next train—and for the occasion that would change them forever.

Declan and Lauren were already standing close to each other on the platform. The crowd knew that there were only a few seconds between the opening and closing of the train car's doors. As soon as these opened, a few people exited the train. And almost immediately, the waiting mass of people on the platform, including Lauren and Declan, got squeezed into what seemed like a single unit, and entered the train. The two of them ended up smack in the middle of the car, face-to-face, and essentially forced into a tight embrace. There was nowhere else to go.

As soon as the train began to accelerate, Declan realized the futility of looking around for a rail or handle to hold on to. He turned his head toward Lauren and met her bewildered eyes. This mutual gaze unexpectedly turned into an extraordinary connection—one that transcended the delightful feeling of Lauren's breath against his shoulder, the gentle awareness of his strong arms successfully isolating her from the constricting mass of people about them, the enchanting sensation of her breasts against his torso, the inevitable contact of their hips, and the thrill of her forehead succumbing by circumstance to rest perfectly on his shoulder. They never realized nor cared how they eventually found themselves at the deep end of the train. As the next rush of passengers boarded, Declan shifted a hand to the nape of her neck and ran his fingers through her hair. She slid her palms to his upper back. Not one word was spoken. Their eyes were closed. Their minds began replaying a sequence of images in which they saw each other in flashing snippets of their recent past:

His preoccupied expression through the kaleidoscope of her tears as sedatives forced her into weeks of oblivion on that crucial night at UTMB. Her beautiful face and delicate, naked body visible through the partially open door as she lay on the bathroom floor. His peculiar smirk and compassionate eyes framed by a background of roses that clear day when they left Galveston together. Her dwindling figure waving goodbye in the rearview mirror the night he drove away from her apartment complex. His strong, agile body, which swiftly lifted up young Max over his shoulders at the airport.

These and many other memories flashed through their minds. Their respective uncertainties about what they meant to each other were finally answered. They felt an uplifting, liberating sensation. Declan no longer believed that fitting the last piece of his puzzle would be unfulfilling. What Lauren once thought was an eternally incomplete puzzle was now a dream come true. They trembled in quiet excitement and anticipation at the realization that they were each other's last piece of the same puzzle.

They reached the end of the line. The train car had emptied completely over a dozen stops. Yet they remained in a frozen embrace, in silent and welcoming acceptance of their undeniable love.

Declan Baltierra and Lauren Madison had never been happier.

—⁊⁊⁊—

Had it not been for a well-mannered man in uniform who pretended to clear his throat, they might have kissed. For the time being, they simply opened their eyes, slowly parted, and smiled at each other—acknowledging their new relationship. Declan begged the subway attendant's pardon, and they both walked off the train, hand in hand, into a significantly more tranquil station.

They eventually reached the National Medical Center. The exit stairway led them to the main lobby of the medical complex. The colossal atrium was reminiscent of a convention center. People dispersed from the stairway in every direction. As the crowd thinned and Declan and Lauren walked farther inside the atrium, they gradually had an unobstructed view of a large mural. It was a modern masterpiece created by the famous artist José Chávez Morado as a memorial of the tragic 1985 Mexico City earthquake. It was also a commemoration of the heroic population who came together to toil for days, saving over 2,300 victims, and then for years thereafter to resurrect a completely leveled hospital into one of the most modern medical complexes in the world.

Lauren gazed in awe at the image of a faceless couple. She felt the man's quiet despair as he sat on a pile of rubble. A woman, presumably his wife, stood firmly behind, touching his shoulders in a comforting gesture. A round sign in relief was superimposed on the left side of the mural. On it was inscribed the date and time of the tragedy: 0719 hours, 19 September 1985. Declan had seen this mural many times. He still felt a curious satisfaction at the scenes depicting rescue personnel and everyday citizens lifting victims and carrying them toward the gloved hands and masked faces of surgeons. Lauren saw a shared dedication in the similar faces of the men and women as they tried to save each other with their bare hands.

"It never fails to stir the hearts and minds of those who are lucky to stand before this amazing piece of art," David Baltierra said. He'd walked up from behind and casually wedged himself between Declan and Lauren. With his arms on their shoulders, the three of them stood reflecting on various other components of the mural.

David offered Lauren his arm. "Well, I must communicate some good news and some bad news," said the esteemed director of the center as he led his guests toward the cafeteria. "The bad news is that Alberto had to help some folks in Monterrey out of a neurosurgical predicament and left early this morning. He will not be joining us for lunch."

"When is he coming back?" Declan asked.

"He will be there only a day, but he's leaving the following day directly to Boston for a conference."

"Perhaps when he retires we can actually spend some time together." Dec shook his head and smiled.

"I don't think he will ever retire. Knowing the professional modus operandi of you two characters, your friendship will forever be confined to email. Anyway, Dec, I'm sorry you won't get to see your college buddy."

"So, what's the good news?" Lauren interjected.

"The good news is that it's seafood bar in the cafeteria. Voilà!" He pointed to a line of people in the large and inviting hospital eatery.

The walls were adorned with works of art. Tables with corresponding dark cherry chairs were set with flowers and uniquely crafted condiment racks. Patrons included medical center staff, visitors, and patients. Soothing ambient music threaded through the hum of innumerable conversations.

As they stood in line, David joked that nobody was quite sure where the seafood actually came from but that at least it was all thoroughly cooked. "It tastes great and it won't kill you. Please, indulge," he said, smiling.

Their nearly hour-long lunch, short by Mexican standards, was amiable. They talked about various subjects. Two of the conversation topics stood out in Lauren's mind. The first revolved around Max's First Communion event. David essentially gave a mini-lecture on the rite of passage and recalled a few funny and borderline embarrassing particulars of Declan's First Communion. One detailed how Dec had delayed the religious ceremony for a considerable amount of time after he refused to recite passages from the catechism until the priest explained why it was necessary to pray to a number of different saints, the Virgin Mary, and the Virgin of Guadalupe.

"I never did get a good answer," Declan said. "But on the upside, I still got that Communion certificate."

"Yes, but it took your mother a while and many coffee and pastry invitations to convince your buddies' parents that you were not a total heathen."

"You mean the heathen I eventually became?" Dec asked.

"Yes, that one."

After a few laughs, Lauren expressed concern that she may not have brought the right clothes for the boy's party. David immediately offered his wife's expertise and suggested that Lauren consult with her.

"That's not a bad idea, but Uncle David, Aunt Tere has a knack for imposing her will in lieu of providing suggestions."

"Dec, you have a point. Come to think about it, I haven't bought anything of my own accord for as long as I can remember. You two better hit the mall immediately."

On that note, they hugged David Baltierra goodbye and opted for a taxi ride to the Santa Fe shopping mall. During the thirty-minute ride, Lauren asked and learned a little more about the second-most-interesting topic of the lunch conversation, Declan's friend Alberto. He was the reason Declan had decided to become a doctor. They had become friends while studying at Yale but, serendipitously, had also met as children many years prior. Unlike Declan's down-to-earth yet privileged upbringing, Alberto had once been an orphaned street child in Mexico City. As a result of a nearly miraculous turn of fate, which was a long and amazing story unto itself, he ended up in the United States and eventually became a neurosurgeon. Their initial encounter had been on a major intersection along Insurgentes Avenue, where Declan and Kate Baltierra would often walk on their way home from his football practices. Alberto had been in a makeshift clown costume, mixing kerosene and water in preparation for the fire-spitting tricks that would support him and his sick aunt. Kate had stopped that notable day to introduce herself and Declan, learn a little about Alberto's life on the street, give him some cash, and have her son shake hands with a child whom, eventually, God or fate would not forsake.

It took months of friendship in college before Alberto hinted at his past to Declan, and they realized that they had met many years before. In time, it was frank admiration for Alberto's dedication to becoming a doctor, rooted in the death of his aunt, which would slowly erode Declan's desire to pursue business.

Declan had also experienced a parallel helplessness—upon the death of his father.

"He was two years ahead of me in college. After he graduated, he went to Harvard Medical School. We kept in close contact while we remained on the East Coast. After I graduated, though, I headed for Texas. Ever since, we have only been able to see each other once in a while. But we've remained good friends."

"Why is he in Mexico?" Lauren asked.

"He recently finished his training in neurosurgery. He stayed on the Harvard faculty for a short time, but he returned to Mexico to serve the people he had promised himself he would serve. He did a lot of research with a focus on removing tumors and cutting out parts of the brain that cause people seizures. That has made him well known."

"Amazing!"

"Yes. He is an amazing person," Declan agreed.

"For sure. But what I meant was that it's almost unbelievable how life weaves these amazing stories together. And that those stories become the origin for yet other surprising stories. For example, what are the chances you and Alberto would meet the way you did, in a city this big, and years later in college? And, you didn't become a doctor because of your uncles. Instead, it was due to your friendship with Alberto." Lauren began to speak progressively slower, reflectively. "Had it not been for the details in that string of events in your life, I may not be here right now, alive, with you."

Declan was about to kiss her.

"Would you like me to let you off at the main entrance or any particular store?" the taxi driver asked as he entered the parking lot of the large shopping complex.

Declan resignedly pulled his attention away from Lauren and addressed the cab driver. "Hey, if you don't mind, why don't you find a parking spot and wait for us. Then you can take us back to Polanco. I will pay you for the entire trip now, and depending on how long you have to wait, you can charge me for your time later. What is your name, by the way? My name is Declan, and this is Lauren."

"My name is Oscar. You don't have to pay me anything now. I trust you. I'll just wait for you here."

As Declan and Lauren walked toward the mall, she said, "When you speak Spanish, you sound so…"

"Mexican?" Dec offered with a smile.

"No-o," Lauren said, pretending to slap his shoulder.

"Amazingly exotic?"

She giggled and added, "Well, yes, but what I was going to say was, hmm, *distinguished.*"

"Oh. Thank you, that's nice."

Declan and Lauren were able to find exactly what she needed for Max's Communion. When they went back to the taxi, Oscar had fallen asleep. Declan lightly squeezed his shoulder through the open window to wake him up.

Soon after hitting the road, traffic became impenetrable. Declan decided to have Oscar drop them off at a subway station. He paid the taxi fare and added just as much in tip. Filled with gratitude, Oscar couldn't help but shake their hands and wish them a good stay in the city.

They headed underground to catch the subway. Once on the train, Declan realized that to go directly to Polanco on the Metro, they would have to transfer to a different subway line at a busy transfer station. Shopping bags in hand, he thought it would be best to avoid that. So, he decided to get off at the Pink Zone stop. There, they'd catch a quick taxi ride home. Besides, it was almost dinnertime, and he remembered a rickety-looking restaurant in the area that served the most outstanding burgers.

The Pink Zone was an area of hotels, restaurants, and other businesses located adjacent to the city's financial center. He and Lauren weaved past a number of nice-looking tourist traps and soon found the burger place—a cart, really, ensconced between two unassuming parking lots. They had a wonderful dinner there, chatting with the other patrons under the rapid-fire commentary of a televised soccer game.

On the way to catch a taxi to the Polanco district, they had to cross Reforma Avenue at the traffic roundabout that encircled the Angel of Independence. Declan thought it prudent to take Lauren to see the monument known around the world as the symbol of Mexico City.

They climbed two dozen steps leading to the base of the twelve-story Corinthian-style column, which supported the golden statue of an angel. The angel held a laurel wreath high with one hand and a broken chain with the other. Lights reflected brilliantly from the stone.

"It was inaugurated at the turn of the century," Declan said. "It was supposed to commemorate independence from Spain a hundred years prior. The four statues of women at the vertices of the entire structure represent Peace, War, Law, and Justice. That statue of a lion led by a child over there reflects the strength necessary during times of war and the docile character of people in times of peace.

"People gather here during demonstrations and to celebrate—usually whenever the national soccer team wins a big game. Traffic shuts down completely. What even most Mexicans don't realize, though, is that in essence, this is actually a mausoleum. The bodies of prominent heroes of the independence movement are buried here. Let me show you something." He led her around the pedestal. "To commemorate these heroes, there is an eternal flame right there, behind the stone. It's tiny, and most people don't know it's there unless they actually take the time to read all the plaques. My dad once told me that the flame used to be plainly visible but that disrespectful pranksters used to throw water at it and constantly turn it off. Anyway, this has always been a very meaningful place for me. Despite the fact that I am a proud American, this site is the symbol of my roots and of the people from this other country that I also love. So, I promised my dad that I would only show the flame to people who were special to me and who would respect and love it like I do."

"How many people have you shown it to?" Lauren asked quietly, taking in everything Declan had just shared.

"One," he said, then they both gently turned toward each other, and their lips came together in a no-longer-elusive first kiss.

TWENTY-THREE

One of the most difficult facts of life is coming to terms with the question of whether all things, good or bad, must come to an end. Or does everything simply become a new beginning?

Aunt Teresa was far from upset when Declan and Lauren didn't eat their meals at home. It became impossible to contain her excitement, and she called Kate in Houston on Friday. She reported that without a doubt, the couple's friendship had evolved—even David and Don Manuel agreed that it had leapt into a romance. They had visited some of the city's best restaurants, spent time at the zoo, and had gone for a boat ride at the lake. Kate could not hold back tears of joy when Teresa assured her that Declan seemed extraordinarily happy—a happiness that Kate knew had eluded her son all his life.

On Saturday morning, Declan refused to let Tere's service staff prepare breakfast. He took it upon himself to get up early and whip up a frying pan full of delicious chilaquiles, a stack of strawberry pancakes, and a large bowl of fresh fruit. The first one to join him was his uncle.

"Wow!" David exclaimed as he slid onto a stool at the kitchen island. He helped himself to the grapefruit juice.

"If you are hungry, dive in," Declan said, placing the dirty dishes in the washer.

"I forgot how good you can be in the kitchen. That apron suits you well, man."

"That's because he learned a great deal from me, isn't that right, Dec?" Teresa asked proudly as she entered the kitchen in one of her usual immaculate outfits. In a mildly castigating tone, she told her husband, "David, we have guests. I know Declan is no problem, but you've got to go rid yourself of those appalling pajamas before Lauren joins us."

"Aunt Tere, I don't think Lauren cares either," Declan told her with a smile.

"Well, I do," Teresa said firmly and nudged David.

While David remained on the stool, contemplating whether to go change, Teresa went around to give Declan a hug and a kiss. "I gave your mother such a hard time for being useless in the kitchen, but I am so glad to know that you learned something from me. I'm really proud of you, Dec."

"Virgin of Guadalupe!" David exclaimed when he caught a glimpse of Lauren approaching the kitchen. "Dear, I am definitely not worthy. I should have listened to my wife, who always knows best. I will be back momentarily." He gently held Lauren's shoulder and gave her a traditional Latin kiss on the cheek.

Lauren had gotten herself ready for Max's First Communion celebration, which would start that afternoon. Knowing that this would begin with a religious ceremony and that they would not have time to go back home to change for the evening festivities, she and Declan had picked a striking blouse, elegantly contoured black pants, and new shoes. The shoes were a treat—two-tone Regina Romero heels with ankle straps.

Not counting the time at UTMB, Declan had never seen her out of a ponytail or with a fully made-up face. He was bewildered.

"Lauren, you look—beautiful."

"That's because she *is* beautiful," Teresa added.

"Oh, I feel so self-conscious. Thank you both," Lauren said, feeling ambivalent about the compliment.

"Honey, we are just making a simple observation of fact. Stop feeling awkward, and come eat some of the good stuff Dec prepared for us. By the way, that whole thing with David was that he should have listened to me when I told him that his pajamas were atrocious."

"Oh, he didn't have to go change for me."

"Okay, maybe he didn't, but it's good for him to do what I say. So don't feel bad," Teresa conceded with a smile and a wink.

A more presentable David soon joined them, and everyone had brunch. Shortly after, Lauren and Declan were on their way in David's silver BMW 530.

Saturday afternoons and most of the day on Sundays were the only times when driving in the greater metropolitan area was actually pleasant. Traffic, the corresponding smog, and the daily masses of people were depleted. The strangely quiet streets adopted a rare vitality that allowed the city to sigh and reminisce on its former splendor and tenacious beauty. The sky was blue for a change. Fountains, trees, flowers, and even parks materialized like holograms. For those newly in love, the clarity and ambiance was all the more vivid.

"You realize this is all very much a dream for me," Lauren told Declan.

"I know what you mean," he said. "I'm just glad it's all very much real."

TWENTY-FOUR

As he had done many times before, Declan saw his enduring hometown steadily dwindle as the plane gained altitude. In the past he had always felt an odd sense of melancholy when the topography below was no longer visible. This time, the feeling just wasn't there. He perceived a certain contentment that could only be explained by the warmth of Lauren's head resting on his shoulder as she gazed through the same double-paned window.

She seemed to stare at the monotonous clouds, but her mind was caught on the images of a church full of people, an ecstatic boy whose smile reflected an uncontainable joy, and a congested dance floor that at times felt like it was her and Declan's private venue.

Staring at the same sky, Declan also slipped into silent recollections. He thought about how out of place his uncle's car had looked parked in front of the church in the Nezahualcóyotl district. That part of the city was affectionately called Neza and was generally thought of as Mexico City's garbage disposal. It was the location of most of the city's landfills and trash processing centers. It was associated with loathsome smells, murky land, unrecognizable debris, gloomy streets, and poverty. But unlike the out-of-place car, Declan and Lauren were very much in place among the families and their plentiful food, drink, music, and rich fellowship.

After the mass, Max's friends and family had convened at a simple, spacious, immaculately decorated gathering hall just a few blocks from the church. Lauren and Declan danced with Max and his extended family, in between helpings from the table of bountiful chicken, beans, rice, and sweets served on paper plates. Along with everyone else, they enjoyed a variety of music, which included *cumbias*, traditional children's songs and melodies, *danzones*, and *trio* music. Above all, they cherished their dances together, as an inseparable unit that, in the eyes of everybody who affectionately glanced at them, only added another dimension to an occasion that was already full of love.

Most of the children tired out before midnight. Lauren draped her arm over Declan's shoulder as she sat comfortably on his lap. Several couples sat in similar positions around the various tables, just listening to the music—either too inebriated or too exhausted to continue dancing. It was at that moment that one of Max's cousins snapped a Polaroid picture of them.

He handed the still-developing photo to Lauren. After having reached into a knapsack, he also gave them another picture of Declan and Lauren in front of the church alongside Max and his family. "A souvenir of this day," he told them.

The third seat in their row was unoccupied, and Lauren was able to lie down and rest her head on Declan's lap. In turn, he reached for a book he had placed in the front seat pocket upon boarding. From within its pages, Declan produced and stared at the two Polaroid pictures. He recalled the final, honest, strong handshake of Max's father, whose waving hand grew infinitely smaller in the rearview mirror as they drove away. He reflected on the prolonged kiss he'd shared with Lauren as they stopped before a red light in the middle of a dark Neza street. And just like that, Max's role in their life had come to a pleasant end.

In those shadowy and imperfect Polaroid images, Lauren seemed almost luminous. Declan then replaced the pictures and the book in front of him. He gently ran his fingers through her hair, closed his eyes, and quietly rejoiced.

—∞—

"Babe? I don't like the way you are pausing like that," Frank said. "Please tell me it's just because you are tired. Crap! Something bad happens, doesn't it?"

"Well, do you want to know what happened next, or should we stop here?"

"Yeah, stop. Wait, no. Go on," Frank said, still looking unsure.

TWENTY-FIVE

D eclan got a call at around two in the morning. He had been back in Galveston for just two days since their trip to Mexico City.

Kate tried to be calm, but her words and tone were hesitant.

"Dec, I'm in the ER at Hermann with Lauren's friend Sandra."

"Is Sandy okay?" he asked.

"Yes. I mean. Well, it's not Sandra. Lauren is the one getting treated."

A chill enveloped Declan. Not unlike a computer, he began to process the possible medical reasons that could have caused Lauren to be ill. Occam's razor was always a good rule of thumb in medicine, so the first thing he surmised was that she had to be suffering some gastrointestinal malady related to the trip. In the back of his mind, he could not rule out a rare complication from her operation.

It was neither.

"Son, I've already talked to Barry Jones in the ER. He overlooked the whole family-only privacy situation after I told him you were her doctor." Kate let out an uncomfortable sigh. "He told me she was, um, *overdosed*."

"Overdosed? On what? She is not on any—"

Kate's voice faltered. "It was a street drug."

There was a long silence on both sides of the phone line. It permeated mother and son with burning pain and perplexity. Unanswerable questions poured into a bottomless pit within their minds. *What did we do wrong? What happened?* Their momentary silence was full of the same questions.

Kate delicately broke the impasse. "Will you come and see her, Declan? We can sort it all out in time. She has just been sedated, but according to Barry, she's medically stable."

Declan told his mother he would be there as soon as he could.

——

Flanked by the myriad lights illuminating innumerable industrial exhaust towers on each side of the Texas City highway, Declan abruptly pulled his Mercedes onto the access road. He stared at the dark and empty space ahead of him for minutes on end. Finally, he picked up his cell phone and dialed Kate. He spoke to her briefly.

"But Dec, it was just a relapse," she said. "We don't know the whole story. Perhaps you should come and find out. Please, son, don't let this go."

Parked on the access road of that deserted highway, Declan sat in his car scrutinizing his actions of the recent past and contemplating what to do now.

Then he made a statement in a tone that Kate identified as final—the kind that Kate knew she would have to respect.

"I know, Mother. I'm sorry. I have been confused about what she means to me. The whole situation seemed straightforward for a short while. But it's evidently more complex than I thought. Maybe it's just me. I don't know. I just don't want to hurt her or see her hurt. If it's me in some way causing that, I cannot be a part of it. Please tell her she is in good hands with the doctors at Hermann."

"And that you don't want to see her again?" she asked.

"And that I have to be in Galveston," Declan corrected her.

There was not much else to say but a mutual "I love you" and goodbye.

Declan felt responsible for Lauren's fate, present and future. He had fallen in love with and established an arguably unethical relationship with a former patient. He had saved Lauren's life and possibly, though unintentionally, might have coerced her not only to leave the hospital with him but also to accompany him to Mexico. He had placed her in social situations that might have been uncomfortable and beyond her ability to cope. He might have instigated in her a sea of confusing emotions and reactions that could have resulted from nothing more than a feeling of indebtedness.

He thought that Lauren had overcome her addiction, but now he realized that she had needed to remain in a more structured therapeutic environment.

He had potentially altered fate and hampered her ability to determine her own life.

Despite innumerable other uncertainties, despite the pain, at that moment, Declan truly believed that letting go was the best thing to do—for Lauren's sake.

⸺⁓∭⁓⸺

That chapter of Declan's life ended immediately after he heard Kate say goodbye. Yet for a while afterward, Declan still held his cell phone to his ear. As if still talking to his mother, through the now deafening silence, he whispered into a toneless phone, "… and that I love her as I've never loved anyone before."

He eventually crossed the highway's shallow median and went back to his life on Galveston Island.

T W E N T Y - S I X

Many seasons passed in the blink of an eye. Declan Baltierra, now a fully credentialed and sought-after cardiothoracic surgeon, found himself headed east on I-95, en route to New Haven, Connecticut. Save for a peculiar receptacle in the back footwell and a plush pillow on the front passenger seat, he did not pack anything more than what could fit in his trunk.

After all this time, he had ended up with Blossom, and together, they were on their way to a new life at Yale.

"And shortly after, Declan and his cat got to New Haven. You sort of know the rest," I told Frank.

"The company of a cat is like a strange, often sporadic, but authentic sort of love…"

"Oh, Frank. How poetic of you."

"Well, there was more to it, but I don't remember the rest. I saw it on a plaque at the pet store."

On that note, Frank and I went to bed.

The next morning, he asked me how long it had been between the last time Declan saw Lauren and the arrival of the package.

I calculated about five years.

TWENTY-SEVEN

Routine is harmless. But it's tricky. It can look a lot like stability. This, in turn, can mask unhappiness. Thankfully, fate is dynamic and has a knack for exacting change.

Tuesdays and Thursdays were especially fulfilling in Declan's new routine at Yale. As part of his incentive to join the medical school faculty, he was allowed to teach undergraduates at the college as well. This was an old dream of his, and it had come true. The perks of being in demand! The med school people wanted so much to ensure his happiness that they gave Declan the autonomy to teach whatever he wanted and work part-time on clinic days. Consistently, he was out the clinic door by late morning.

This allowed him to go home, collect Blossom, and head out to lunch. He and the cat had become a fixture around campus. They were seemingly inseparable. During a trip to Mexico just before he left Texas, he'd visited the leather shop of Carlos Rueda in Villa del Carbón—a picturesque town outside Mexico City. He'd commissioned a custom satchel with a perfectly contoured orifice in the middle of the top flap. It had two handles and a shoulder strap. He could comfortably fit the cat in the main compartment and still have room for papers and even a book. Looking like a furry periscope, Blossom would travel with her head through the opening and enjoy the sights and sounds of New Haven. And if she ever got scared or bored, she'd simply drop down and sleep inside the satchel.

Among many places he could choose for lunch, Declan was partial to the cafeteria at the graduate school of business. From the time he was an undergraduate, they still seemed to serve the best sandwiches around. And it was yet another of the many establishments where the management did not seem to mind his unobtrusive companion. Welcoming his faithful pet in public spaces had become the norm, as Declan had evolved into one of the most recognized professors at Yale.

The first semester of Anatomy and Physiology 126ab, eventually dubbed "Lay's Anatomy," he taught in a dusty classroom in the basement of Osborn Memorial Laboratories. Unlike the imposing, pristine brown brick building that housed it, his classroom was dilapidated. It had obviously been overlooked during the multimillion-dollar renovation a few years prior. Its walls were crumbly and adorned with large, geographically shaped splotches of water damage. The smell was a mixture of damp forest with a hint of barnyard, probably owing to the laboratory animals next door. The desks were the traditional hard, dark oak, uncomfortable vestiges of former generations. The presence of those generations was preserved in the benchtop inscriptions. On seat 22, there was a barely discernible name carved on the wood, which seemed to read *Gell-Mann '48*. An age-smeared one on the top of desk 12 read *Fucking war*. It could have been any war including or after WWI. And on and on, a century's worth of history endured in the graffiti left over by generations of bored students.

Only fourteen of the twenty seats were safe to sit on. That first semester, only twelve people showed up. After the end of the class-shopping period, only ten of those students officially registered for Declan's course. Unpredictably, spring semester brought in twenty-three students, some of whom sat, perhaps more comfortably, on a long lab bench in the back of the room.

The class was not a hard-core science course. Declan's goal was to provide a broad understanding of human anatomy and some pertinent, common disease processes that would make even the least science-inclined students knowledgeable about the subject. He felt certain that even future stockbrokers or journalists would find use in knowing about the human body and how it worked.

Declan used Frank Netter's atlas as the basis for the class. But Declan presented the material in multiple ways, including X-rays, gross specimens he borrowed from the medical school, three-dimensional computer graphics, and even concepts that ranged from electrical circuits to plumbing.

Thanks to his charisma, his dynamic lecture style, and the fact that students truly gained a surprisingly strong understanding of the human body, the course quickly gained popularity. The third semester became a standing-room-only situation with forty-seven students.

His class was initially created as a favor to Declan's boss at the medical school.

Declan's boss, a professor emeritus of surgery, had paid a friendly visit to the dean of Yale College before Declan had even arrived in New Haven. Over tea, he'd told him, "Boyd, don't worry. When my boy sees that his little teaching fling here in the college is not worth it or when he eventually gets bored doing it, he'll pull out and you can take it off your curriculum."

"You must really need this fellow to give him that kind of leeway," said Boyd Patterson, who fully expected Declan's class to fail. He'd honestly thought that someone without teaching experience would not last a minute in front of some of the brightest and most demanding students in the country.

The venerable surgeon had answered, "Indeed. Baltierra is a superb and innovative surgeon. And I like him as a person too. So yes, I need him on the medical school faculty. To me, though, he belongs in the classroom I call the operating room, training other surgeons. But a happy guy is a better surgeon, so if he wants to come down this way and write on a chalkboard every now and then, so be it. At any rate, I really do appreciate you helping me do this for him."

"Well, until he decides to stay exclusively on your side of the tracks, we'll take good care of him," the dean concluded.

—m.—

They did a whole lot more than take good care of him.

In the spring of his second year, Declan was teaching in a large classroom in the center of campus at the gothic yet modern W. L. Harkness Hall. The administration initially surmised that his Lay's Anatomy was a "soft" class and that students might be taking it because it was an easy science credit. After various marginally covert audits of his class by faculty, Boyd Patterson ultimately deemed it to be, as the official report put it, "in tune with the tradition of academic excellence of the college and, quite simply, fabulous!"

Declan was promptly extended all the courtesies given to Yale College faculty. He was given an official faculty appointment, separate from the one he held at the medical school, and was offered a fellowship to Silliman, one of the twelve residential colleges on campus. In the spring of his third year, he received a phone call that preempted a formal letter with the same information. Dean Patterson informed him that the interest in his class had exceeded not only the seating capacity of Harkness Hall but also his formerly erroneous expectations—for which he kindly apologized. Furthermore, he told Dec that rather than limiting the number of students who could take the class, he would make arrangements to have Battell Chapel available for the upcoming semester.

"Congratulations, Dr. Baltierra. As you know, there are other large auditoriums on campus, but lecturing at Battell is an honor that has been given to a select number of professors over the school's storied history," Dean Patterson said. "A unanimous vote to extend you the privilege of imparting your lectures at Battell has been taken by myself and the few other gray-haired individuals you may have occasionally noticed snooping around in your classroom."

He continued, "In the meantime, we have used this little vote as an excuse to have the university pay for an expensive dinner and hard alcohol at Beinecke Library on Friday. You are the main attraction, and we will expect you at around six for cocktails."

"Thank you," Declan stammered in disbelief.

"You are welcome. Enjoy the rest of your day. Cheers."

Declan turned to Blossom, who was sitting next to him on the couch, and said, "You are moving up in the world, kid."

—⁂—

While he sensed and was aware of his popularity, he remained fundamentally unaffected. In fact, he was generally oblivious to the day-to-day admiration as he interacted with people around him. He attributed most of the attention to having Blossom poking out of his satchel everywhere or having her lounge on his classroom desk. The cat would often identify a consenting student in the front row and curl up on his or her lap for the duration of a lecture. Not surprisingly, the front rows were often occupied by attractive female students, who fought comically over Blossom's attention at the beginning of each class. None of them, however, got any more or less attention from Declan than the students at the back of the room.

When he wasn't out and about on the college campus, his routine at the medical school was as straightforward as it had always been. There were many interesting challenges, but work in clinic, the operating room, conferences, short lectures, and seminars were ordinary and bordering on mundane. Notwithstanding this fact of his life, he still enjoyed being an academic surgeon. Socially, he had acquired a loosely knit group of friends good for occasional parties, picnics, meals, movies, and so on. Nothing or no one, though, could penetrate the invisible shield that seemed to separate him from all romantic relationships. He was convinced that he did not want or need a romance that lasted more than a weekend. Declan felt settled, professionally fulfilled, financially secure, and generally content. "What else could I ask for?" he would respond to friends and family when they seemed worried.

Of course, the last thing he asked for was a nosy but loving secretary.

The status quo had reached an impasse.

TWENTY-EIGHT

The exact date I chose was inconsequential. Only that it happened a couple of weeks after I mailed that crucial letter to the sender of the package. It was a chilly, colorful spring day. The time was exactly 1:00 p.m. The place was a capacity-filled Battell Chapel. The previously selected numbered seat was in the center of the balcony's first row, directly in front of the pulpit.

There she sat, with heart racing and expectant eyes. Her clammy hands clutched the mahogany box I had left for her at the hotel the night before. By then, I was certain she had understood the letter I had initially sent her. This time, along with the box, I left her another simple message: *This remarkable package is best delivered in person.*

Her elegant and contemporary apparel made even the best-dressed students around her look grungy. She had taken off a beige, fitted, quilted jacket. Her exquisite body was contoured to perfection by a black, long-sleeve, crewneck shirt accented with Burberry check trim at the shoulders and small side pockets. The jacket on her lap lay over caramel-colored, wool, straight-leg pants that in turn discreetly revealed a pair of stylish, square-toed heels with matching check piping. She seemed straight out of the pages of *Vogue*.

What kept students around her, male and female alike, constantly gazing at her in fascination was not just her pristine attire but her graceful beauty. The fundamental loveliness of her natural features was further complemented by perfectly styled, just-below-the-shoulder raven hair; meticulous attention to detail in the almost professional application of her makeup; flawlessly shaped brows and lashes that brought out a pair of gleaming brown eyes; and a general air of chic sophistication. In short, Lauren Madison was breathtaking.

———

That day, Declan arrived a few minutes late. He had to contend with a particularly chaotic road construction crew outside. This forced him to take a brief detour and chain his bike half a block farther away than usual.

Lauren gasped softly when she saw him enter. He placed his satchel on the table next to the pulpit.

She tried to contain the explosive, myriad memories of their time together and the pent-up feelings she had for him. Almost simultaneously, she noticed Blossom slothfully exiting the leather case. The cat stretched and eventually lay down on the table. Just before he dimmed the overhead lights, it happened—or so she thought.

Declan glanced in every direction, adjusting the microphone on his collar. He gave a brief introduction of the day's topic. When the path of his vision shifted in her direction, Lauren tensed. Her heart sped up, and her thoughts froze. Before her, once again, were the powerful yet gentle eyes of the man who had changed her life and whom she still loved above all else.

Suddenly, the lights turned off and gave way to a projected image of a bottle of Jack Daniel's superimposed on an extracted human liver. The lecture proceeded *almost* routinely.

Lauren felt baffled and disillusioned. She didn't know if Declan had seen her. This uncertainty made her uneasy.

———

While overjoyed to be teaching in such a large venue, Declan was not particularly fond of having to use a microphone. He also disliked the fact that it was much darker in Battell Chapel than a classroom with normal windows. The bright light emanating from the projector behind his audience often blinded him sporadically during his lectures, but he made do.

Perhaps only a surgeon, accustomed to the automatic suppression of emotion, could have maintained such composure that day in the face of such an extreme shock.

He had, indeed, seen Lauren.

During a discussion of biliary and pancreatic juices, portal veins, and how a molecule of ethanol passes through cell membranes, he struggled internally. *Is that really her? Why is she here? What should I do? How do I face the woman I may have wrecked—the woman I may have brusquely abandoned—the woman I'm still trying to forget—the woman I love?* Declan's thoughts reeled. *The woman I love*, he told himself again and again.

Minutes later, and just before flashing another slide of anatomic diagrams, his mind succumbed. Declan paused his lecture and switched on the chapel's lights. He adjusted his eyes and fixed them directly ahead to the balcony, where he had seen her.

Lauren was gone.

Utter silence pervaded the hall. Hundreds of students focused mutely on Declan as he walked across the middle aisle toward the balcony. He stood below, gawking up at the empty seat. The students flanking it looked at each other and down at their commanding but perplexed professor.

A young man seated by the door rose to his feet and scurried to Declan's side. "Here, Dr. Baltierra. This was left for you." Declan accepted the beautiful mahogany box from the student and proceeded to open it.

One of the chapel's lights beamed down on a dazzling platinum medallion within. The masks of comedy and tragedy were depicted in relief. The medallion was mounted on a semilunar frame that rested on a gleaming black pedestal. The engraved plaque read *American Theatre Wing—Tony Award.*

He reached for the trophy with his hand. Declan was even more confused. He continued to stare at the glossy trophy, but then noticed the student in front of him examining the back of the object. Declan turned the trophy over and realized there was another inscription on the reverse side of the medallion:

THE LEAGUE OF

NEW YORK THEATRES

AND PRODUCERS, INC.

PRESENTS TO

Lauren Alexis Madison

Best Leading Actress in a Play

The Citadel

Then he noticed a card in the box. On it was a rose garden that looked a lot like the one at UTMB. He picked up the card, flipped it open, and read the message:

To my Angel of Independence,

Please add this trophy to the countless others you must surely have. It is legitimately yours.

Thank you.

Declan again held the Tony Award in front of him and stared at it with bewilderment and earnest admiration. He trembled as he reread her full name inscribed on the medallion. At that moment, Declan knew with irrefutable clarity that there had never been an escape from his utter love for Lauren. There was nothing else to think about or do in that instant but to run after the last piece of his nearly perfect life puzzle.

"Please, hold this and look after my cat. I have to go for a moment," he asked of the student standing next to him. Declan's heart beat with new energy. He sprinted toward the door, briefly turning around to his large audience, and blissfully shouted, "Class dismissed!"

He rushed out, down a set of steps, and then paused at the corner of Elm and College. He looked in every direction, over a conglomeration of machinery, heaps of broken pavement, and men in hard hats. Finally, he saw Lauren sitting on a bench in the park across the street—her neck erect, legs elegantly crossed, hands clutching a tissue, and her eyes staring emptily ahead.

He called her name and started walking across the street toward her. He was so thrilled to see her that he didn't notice the No Pedestrians sign in the middle of the sidewalk. And, they would later find out that the construction worker assigned to monitor the area had gotten momentarily distracted.

Lauren saw Declan. Their eyes met at a distance. Her hands suddenly rose to her mouth as if in shock. Simultaneously, the metal bucket of a construction excavator swung around briskly, like the turret of a tank, directly into Declan. He fleetingly sensed the swiveling machine just behind him. But it came at him too fast—he was unable to react. The impact on his upper body was severe.

For Declan, the light of day was no more.

TWENTY-NINE

Just over five years ago, Kate Baltierra had held Lauren's hand as she came out of her drug overdose that night in the emergency room at Houston's Memorial Hermann. Sandy stood on the opposite side of the gurney with a hesitant smile when Lauren's eyes opened.

Lauren looked around the room, registered the environment, and realized her situation. Tears welled in her eyes. After a moment, it became evident that Declan did not and was not going to come.

"Lauren, I am awfully sorry," Kate said, breaking the silence.

"Please, don't be." Lauren sat up. Speaking to both, she said, "You being here means the world to me. It's pointless for me to explain anything. My weaknesses and my confusion, though—they end here. Kate, I cherish your friendship so much. But if you don't mind, I would also like to ask that you leave me here alone with Sandy."

"Leave now? Are you sure?" Kate asked with genuine concern.

"Yes," Lauren said. She leaned over and gave Kate a firm hug and a kiss on the cheek.

"What about Blossom?" Kate asked.

"Since she is already at your house, I'd like you to keep her."

Sandy had come around to help support Lauren on the bed.

Reluctantly, Kate moved away, and just before their hands unclasped, Lauren vowed to her, "I promise you that, despite this, your efforts have not been in vain."

Kate knew this last statement also referred to Declan. With tears in her eyes, she blew Lauren a motherly kiss and gave her an honest smile. "I know, dear, and…" She paused before closing the door behind her. "He knows too."

Lauren checked out of the ER, and Sandy took her home. On the way to their apartment, she begged her friend not to question what she was planning to do and apologized for having to back down from their plan to move to the new apartment.

"If Kate calls, just tell her that I have to get away. Tell her that I couldn't bear to be a disappointment to them and to myself. Tell her that I have to go and find myself, that maybe one day I will deserve their wonderful friendship. And let her know that I will always, always love her and Declan and Blossom."

Then Lauren related to Sandy what had happened the night she and Declan had returned from Mexico.

Once in their apartment, Lauren packed her small duffel and left Houston.

———

The night Declan and Lauren returned from Mexico, her brother and sister-in-law had been waiting in their car just outside the apartment building. Sandy had not yet arrived home from work. They waited until Declan left and then knocked on Lauren's door.

She rushed to the door, certain it was Declan with an encore kiss.

"Oh! Hello, Perry. Libby?" Lauren was bewildered and profoundly disappointed.

"Yes. It's us, you little junkie," Libby said with an exuberant, chastising drawl as she let herself into the living room. "Who is the john in the Mercedes? Your last trick?" She yanked open the fridge door. "Do you keep anything to drink in this refrigerator? My God, Perry, look, she even has vegetables and milk!" Libby's humor was like steam from a dragon's mouth. She grabbed a can of Diet Coke and popped it open.

Lauren imagined a stream of sizzling smoke from Libby's mouth rising as the belligerent woman drank from the can.

"What brings you guys to Houston?"

Libby smiled, but it was more like a baring of her fangs.

"You have the gall to ask, you little shit? What 'brings' us here is *you*, of course. I couldn't care less, really, but Perry here has been worried sick. God knows why he gives a crap about you. Right after we last saw you in Victoria, it seems you had to come right back here to get your filthy drugs. All this time we thought you were in jail, where you belong, if you ask me. If it wasn't for Sandy's mother, who told us you were living in this place and begged me to check on you two drifters, we wouldn't be here wasting our time. So, anyway, what do you have to say for yourself?"

"Well, I'm clean. I have a job. I live in this apartment, which isn't much but it's decent. We might be moving to a nicer place soon. I'm thinking about returning to school too. And I am sorry I didn't tell you, but like you said, I didn't think you cared. Sandy is also doing well and has continued to go to college. As far as I know, she sends her mother money and gifts. So, we are fine, really. Oh, and I have a boyfriend. His name is Declan. He is a doctor."

"Right!" Libby snapped. "I can guess how a junkie hick girl can get herself a sugar daddy."

Lauren was beginning to feel distressed, as she had felt so many times in the past when overpowered by Libby. Her brother, as usual, stood in silence, seemingly devoid of emotion and blindly compliant to his wife's arguments. Perry had allowed himself to be robbed of self-esteem and individuality a long time ago. Lacking any semblance of support at that instant and exhausted by the whirlwind of recent events in her life, Lauren was unable to turn off the loud admonishments in her mind.

"Does he even know you are a drug addict?"

"Libby, I told you. I no longer use. And yes, he knows I was a junkie. He actually helped me clean up. He loves me, Libby."

"Get a grip! And you think he's going to want you when he finds out you turned tricks for drugs? Don't think I don't know. Bobby Joe told me the last time you were back home you slept with anyone who could spare a dollar bill. He even showed me a picture of you at Deuces Tavern with everyone's hands all over your bare tits. Bobby Joe would have married you, you know? He stands to inherit the movie theater. But you screwed that up. He told me that after seeing you like that, there was no way he could ever be with such a slut. Who knows what else or who else you did for your shit here in Houston."

Lauren's legs gave out, and she sank to the cold linoleum floor, unable to hold back a sob. "He doesn't have to know. You don't have to say anything, Libby. Please."

"Not me, honey. It's just a fact. Somehow, these sorts of things come out one way or another." She shrugged indifferently. "The way I see it, I'm helping you out here. Think about it. Some man like that with the likes of you? You think he's going to marry you? I don't think so. You are just a little sideshow before he marries a proper woman. Maybe he already is married—it just don't seem right to me. Perry, tell her."

There wasn't a sound out of the emotionally stunted man.

"Fine. I guess we've done our duty to see about the two of you. I've said my piece. You take care now. I guess we wouldn't mind if you called to show us a sign of life sometime. And for what it's worth, you should think about going back to where you belong. I still think Bobby Joe could probably find a way to like you, especially looking all nice like that. Anyway, Perry, let's go, we have a long ride back."

The couple left as swiftly as they had shown up—like a tsunami—leaving behind immeasurable damage.

Lauren could not think straight. Her soul felt trapped in the past and its tangle of awful truths. *What if Dec finds out?* she wondered. *How could I ever face him?* She felt disoriented and wobbly, despite being on the floor.

What she didn't know was that Declan would have loved her just the same. He was anything but naïve—he knew how addiction made people desperate, and he knew what desperate people did. He accepted Lauren with his eyes open, from the moment he met her as a patient to the moment he declared his love for her that night under the angel statue and its eternal flame.

Lauren did not see it that way. What her eyes saw in that instant was a partially open apartment door. She stumbled up and ran out to catch a bus in search of the only kind of relief she could think of.

When she rang the once familiar doorbell at a shady unit in the projects, her intention was to ask for a downer. She was hoping it would calm her and let her think logically. Yet once inside, any scrap of rational thought ceased to exist. She succumbed to the environment. The next time Lauren perceived any light, it was on an ambulance, as paramedics checked her pupillary reflexes, on the way to Hermann.

After that episode, Lauren never touched a street drug again.

THIRTY

Lauren's improbably expeditious yet prodigious journey to Radio City Music Hall and eventually to that park bench across from Battell Chapel began at a Greyhound bus station in Houston. She was still wearing her hospital wristband when she bought a ticket to Pittsfield, Massachusetts. It was almost dawn. Cleaning crews traversed the waiting area, nearly finished with their shift. The next shift was already arriving. A few of them, obviously fresh out of bed and fully caffeinated, began replenishing all kinds of products in the staggering array of vending machines. Sleeping passengers lay scattered and contorted on the benches. Only a handful of would-be travelers sat or stood awake, watching an inaudible TV.

Lauren sat on the same duffel she had taken to Mexico. She rested her elbows on a small backpack in her lap and stared at the two Polaroids that would be her only tangible keepsakes of a fairy tale. An unexpected energy buttressed her broken heart; the photos gave her determination. She would find a way to make her life worthwhile.

It was that spirit that carried her through an essentially miserable road trip. The funk of passengers' body odor lingered in the bus over ten states and nearly two days. This was occasionally interrupted by the aroma of fast food procured at bus transfer points—Mobile, Atlanta, New York City, and Springfield.

At last, Lauren arrived in Pittsfield.

She approached a pay phone still bearing the name of the now-defunct Southern New England Telephone Company. From that point on, anything in her life she would have to make happen for and by herself, even if that first action was to ask for a little help.

What would she tell her aunt? She had not seen her in many years. Save for the sporadic cards Lauren had received on her birthdays and some holidays, her ties to her mother's sister were all but severed. She held an old birthday card and unfolded it to the message inside. What if the telephone number written there didn't work? Would she try to make her way to the address, now age-smeared on the face of the purple envelope? What if the aunt who had once told Lauren that she loved her now rejected her after all these years without communication?

In the time it took Lauren to deposit fifty cents and dial the number, a sudden certitude eclipsed all her unanswerable questions. Whatever happened, with or without her aunt's help, she would make do.

The phone number worked.

And fortunately, her astonished aunt still loved Lauren very much. Twenty minutes later, the white Subaru Outback had not even come to a complete stop when Alexis Taylor flung open the passenger door, hastily walked away from the car, and promptly threw her arms around Lauren. In the first few seconds of their embrace, Lauren felt as though she was hugging a stranger. But an instant later, wordless tears affection bonded the kindred women.

"Robert, come here. Remember Lauren?"

"Lauren, it's a pleasure seeing you again," Robert said.

"The pleasure is mine. And I am sorry to—"

"Nonsense," Alexis interrupted. "There will be no 'sorries.' Come on, let's go home and have lunch. Catching up is always better with food."

Alexis and Robert's traditional Cape Cod–style house off Newell Street was small but inviting. Except for the outside shutters and inside crown molding, painted a burnt pink, the house was all white. The small front and backyards were landscaped simply with mulch, gravel, and a variety of flowers. The inside of the house was warm and as colorful as the garden. The furniture was no-frills but seemed comfortable. The wooden floor was old but meticulously preserved. The aroma of freshly baked brownies was the only thing that soon upstaged the uncomplicated and pleasant character of their home.

After chatting into the evening, enjoying the brownies around the coffee table, it became evident to Lauren that the only unconventional aspect of the household was a palpable love between her aunt and Robert. Until then, Lauren had always assumed they were married. As it turned out, Alexis informed her, "We never felt it was necessary."

"I guess if you are not married," Robert said, "there is never really the option to get divorced. I know that sounds like a weird concept, but it has only brought us closer over the years."

It was obvious to Lauren that they were good and gracious people. During the course of the evening, both sensed Lauren's fragile state. They felt that by talking about their relationship, past and present, they could convey to her a sense of tranquility and trust.

The couple provided a frank synopsis of how they met and how they came to be so content after almost thirty years together. Lauren learned that they had lost their only child to a heart condition and any prospect of future children to uterine cancer, which was caught early but had required a hysterectomy. All three reminisced about the handful of times the couple had visited Lauren's family in Texas. Lauren remembered that it was during those visits that she was able to put a face to the origin of her middle name.

In between conversation about Robert's towing service business and Alexis's secretarial job at a law firm, they told Lauren that they initially stopped visiting Texas after a silly argument with her mother. Before that, she and Lauren's mother had always been close. And after Lauren's mother died, Libby and Perry had asked them never to visit again. They gave no reasons. Alexis had always wanted to establish a relationship with Lauren, but due to the request and the circumstances of her own life, she and Robert simply lost the connection over time.

The mostly lopsided conversation eventually came to an inevitable halt marked by an uncomfortable silence.

Finally, Lauren said, "Aunt Alex, I know you said no sorries. But I am sure it's obvious that I'm in a bit of a…um, difficult situation, and that I could use a hand and a place to stay very, very briefly. So, I am sorry, but so thankful." The couple nodded in polite silence. Lauren collected her thoughts. "I've found it hard and distracting back home to concentrate on college. I'm in and out of school all the time. Last year I was really close to finishing my basics, but it just didn't work out. A few days ago, I realized it would be impossible to break the cycle I was in and decided to get away from it completely. I thought that a different town, a different college, and maybe different people would be more beneficial. So, I took a chance and hopped on a bus here." She paused again, hoping they were not expecting any more details. Lauren was not ready to share, not now and maybe never, with anyone, the events of her recent past.

"I'd just like to ask for your hospitality until I can find a job. Then, once I'm settled on my own, I want to do whatever it takes to finally get through college. I'm sure there is a school around here where I can finish my basics. And if you two wouldn't mind, I'd really love to have a family relationship with you. Since Mom died, Perry and I have drifted completely apart."

As easily as that, Lauren shifted the conversation, revealed her intentions, and avoided any uncomfortable explanations.

Her new life began early and brightly the next morning. Lauren showered and dressed. Quietly, she cut up cantaloupe, bananas, and strawberries, which she mixed with blueberries and made a fruit salad. After preparing a pot of coffee, she left a note: *I hope this helps start off your weekend. I am off to find a job. Love, L.* She left through the back door, unheard.

She walked all over the relatively small, quaint downtown, familiarizing herself with the streets and buildings. Rather than buying a newspaper and checking the want ads, she figured that looking for Help Wanted signs in windows was a surer way of finding a position. She also reasoned that the sort of minimum-wage employment she was looking for would probably not merit the expense of a newspaper ad.

She was right.

The sign was intentionally tiny. The folks at the Court Square Café needed to replace Andre, a well-liked, hardworking waiter who had recently moved to another city. They knew that the right person for the job would be someone observant enough to notice the sign, and they wanted a person with the initiative to inquire about the job in person.

Lauren approached an aproned woman at the upper end of middle age and introduced herself. "I just moved here yesterday, and I'm out looking for a job. Are you who I should talk to about the sign in the window?"

"I'm Jackie. You've come at a super busy time. And as you can see, we are shorthanded." She kept her voice neutral, with only a hint of friendliness—perhaps on purpose. She gestured for Lauren to give her a second while she saw to a couple of customers who wanted to settle their bill.

Just as Jackie finished with the customers, Lauren told her, "Well, if you don't mind, I'll just fumble around a little with the menu. I'm pretty sure I can figure things out by looking at how everybody else does things. If you have an extra apron, I'll try to make you feel less shorthanded. At the end of the day, you can tell me whether you want me back."

Lauren's frank demeanor worked like an instant charm. That was precisely the kind of response Jackie had been hoping for.

Lauren expertly waited on tables during the breakfast and lunch rushes and helped dispense to-go deli items in between filling up coffee mugs and water glasses. She bused and cleaned and generally helped beyond her role as a waitress. From the moment Lauren had put on an apron, Jackie knew they had found their new employee. Toward the end of the day, Jackie went to the window, picked up the Help Wanted sign, and when she was sure Lauren was watching, smiled at her and tossed the piece of cardboard in the trash.

Lauren mouthed a heartfelt "thank you."

After closing, Lauren went outside and crossed the street. She turned around to look at the reddish-brown, two-story building that housed the popular downtown eatery she had just spent the day working at. The blue awning showed the establishment's name with white letters. By itself, the restaurant and two adjacent businesses seemed bland and reminiscent of an old mill. Just behind the building, she could see a castle-like tower sprouting above. A short distance to the right stood a small, beautiful church with a river rock façade. On the opposite side of the street was an architecturally captivating public library. And in every direction, she could see people of all ages populating the street. Her new place of work and the constellation of sights and sounds immediately around her made her feel like her new life was off to a good start.

—⁓—

Months later, everything that had once looked so picturesque, joyful, and personally fruitful to Lauren had become ordinary. So much so, in fact, that Lauren started to seek more challenges. She had secured a tiny room in a multifamily duplex a short distance from town. Bills for utilities now arrived in her name. She had arranged a deal to begin repayment of her small but long overdue balances with her credit card company. Just a short walk up East Street, she found an additional part-time job at Roses N' Blooms. The cosmopolitan flair and knack for perfection she had gained while working for Kate Baltierra served her well at the small flower shop. And it gave her a second income in her bank account. Lauren spent weekends with Robert and Alexis for meals, movies, and engaging conversation. Come fall, they went shopping for a suitable coat for her first East Coast winter. Her new routine was comfortable; in her mind and heart, however, she was anything but ensconced. There was no settling down for someone so desperately in search of herself.

Lauren did not begin to fulfill that search for a little over a year. That was about the time it took her to finish her basics at Berkshire Community College. She took classes anytime she could, including nights and weekends. After numerous meetings with academic advisers that bordered on begging, Lauren was able to transfer most of her old credits. She wanted so badly to be able to transfer to a four-year college and get a degree.

For a long time, Lauren's days and nights were fully devoted to work and school. She used her little bit of free time to exercise and to see her aunt and Robert.

Days turned into weeks, weeks turned into months, and time simply became a blur—an exceptionally productive one.

THIRTY-ONE

The surprise party took place late one summer. Court Square Café was open Tuesday to Sunday until three p.m. and was closed on Mondays, but Jackie Davy had asked Lauren if she could help do a special cleanup on Monday evening. Lauren agreed without a second thought, even though it wasn't one of their scheduled deep-cleaning days.

Lauren changed into old, grungy clothes and left her apartment, ready to do battle with grime. When she turned the corner from Wendell onto East Street, she noticed Phil Degarmo standing in front of the restaurant, smoking. Phil was the longtime cook. Except for a fairly misanthropic personality, he was a good and reliable friend to the owners and always cordial enough to the handful of employees. Oddly, though, as soon as his skeletal frame turned toward Lauren, he smiled so widely that his bald scalp wrinkled. Phil wore slacks and a dress shirt. Somewhat surprised, Lauren waved back.

"How are you, Lauren?" he asked, flinging an expended cigarette butt onto the sidewalk and casually twisting his Doc Marten over it.

"I'm well, Phil. Thank you. How are you?" Lauren responded.

"I'm good, Lauren, I'm good."

"Hey, I don't think I've ever seen you in anything but white clothes and an apron," Lauren said. "You look too nice for cleaning duty."

"Oh yeah? These are my Sunday best." Phil pretended to adjust his collar.

At that point, Lauren noticed that the restaurant's blinds were closed. She thought that was peculiar, as she had never seen the blinds used. She had an inkling that something odd was going on.

"Uh, Lauren. I was sort of volunteered to, um, bring you in."

"Bring me in?"

"Yeah. I mean—well, you are supposed to close your eyes."

It became obvious to Lauren that she was the subject of whatever was going on, and that it had nothing to do with cleaning. She smiled and gave Phil a hug. Just before she closed her eyes, she caught a glimpse of Phil's flushed but jolly face.

"I always thought you didn't like me," she said.

"Oh, goodness! No. I like you very much," Phil said almost apologetically. "It's just that you always remind me of my daughter. We have not talked in years. I just didn't know how I would feel about it. You know, talking to you and thinking about her and all. It's to do with me—weird me. There's nothing to it."

"So, how does it feel, then?" Lauren asked.

"What?"

"Talking to me," she responded lightheartedly.

"Good, actually," Phil said. "Wanna go in now?"

Lauren extended her hand, which he clasped into his, and he led her inside.

"Surprise!"

Coworkers from both of Lauren's jobs and their families, her employers, a few friends from the community college, her aunt, and Robert were all there. They had gathered to celebrate Lauren's pending departure from Pittsfield and to show her their appreciation for her kind, determined personality.

When most of the various pastas, salads, bite-size sandwiches, and wine had been consumed, Jackie Davy tapped a spoon against an empty glass.

"We have known Lauren for just under a couple of years," Jackie said, standing in the center of the room. "She has not only helped us make our customers happy, but she has become a friend to everyone here. I'm sure the same is true for you folks at the flower shop and pretty much anybody who has had the pleasure to know Lauren. Lauren, honey, you are such a hard worker. We all love your personality and your permanent smile. Oh, and you are so pretty that I'm sure we've been getting extra business from all the people who have a crush on you. So, the business thanks you for that."

The crowd chuckled.

"Anyway, this is not really a goodbye party, because you are not going too far," Jackie continued. "We know you will come see us frequently. Also, please tell all your classmates at MCLA to stop by and eat something on their way to or from the Mass Pike." She raised a white envelope. "Gosh, we've all grown to love and admire you so much—for that and more, we wanted to give you this surprise party and these couple of gifts. This first one is from me and Eddie. It's your salary for the next three weeks. Only, we don't want you to work. Yesterday was your last day. We want you to relax and see the beautiful Berkshires. We would like you to stop working, working, working for a change. Maybe you can even move to your dorm early and just veg out before your classes start. I don't know, just do something nice for yourself."

Jackie's husband, Eddie, handed her another envelope, which she held up in the air. "This second envelope is from everyone else you see here. It's your book fund. I think it may actually cover you for the whole next year, maybe more. And…"

But there was nothing else to say. Lauren had come forward and put her arms around Jackie. She cried as she hugged, kissed, and personally thanked every last person there.

"I'm not good at speeches," Lauren said to the small crowd. "I want you all to know that this means the world to me." She paused to find the right words. "The year before I moved to this wonderful town with all you wonderful people, my life was in a bit of a…a dip, I guess. I know what rock bottom is, to say the least. Luckily, there have been people"—her mind flashed to Galveston, Houston, and Mexico—"people like you, who have been caring enough to throw me a rope and pull me up. Because of that, I now see a future. So, I love you guys. I thank you so much for these." Lauren waved the two envelopes and added, "I promise you that this will go far but will never, ever leave my heart."

Heading off any potentially awkward silence, Phil announced, "Okay, folks, it seems like a good time for the cake I baked!"

Everybody clapped and enjoyed cake and one another's company. All of Lauren's friends eventually went home happy and in great spirits.

THIRTY-TWO

The Massachusetts College of Liberal Arts was located in the quintessentially northeastern town of North Adams. The college was not particularly well known, but it was quite a first-rate institution. It mainly catered to area residents, although there were many students from all over Massachusetts, surrounding states, Canada, and other parts of the country. The school had well-established relationships with several community colleges. Many students generally studied at those institutions for one to two years and then transferred to MCLA to complete a bachelor's degree program. But for at least two years, students who transferred had an opportunity to experience all that a traditional four-year college had to offer. Furthermore, it was a public college with fairly accessible tuition to state residents.

Lauren had secured admission, junior standing, Massachusetts residency, a little financial aid, and a job checking out books at Freel Library. Best of all, she was assigned a single dorm room at Hoosac Hall.

Like the dutiful parents they had come to feel like to Lauren, Robert and Alexis drove her to MCLA that fall. The ride north on Route 7 featured the most fascinating scenery Lauren had ever seen. She couldn't get enough of the rolling hills and ancient trees painted with hues of orange, brown, yellow, green, and cabernet red. The air through the open car windows felt crisp and fragrant. The Berkshires were surreal—a heaven on earth.

Holding on to her energetic spirit and enormous motivation to succeed, Lauren felt almost complete happiness.

From the moment a customer at Court Square Café told Lauren about MCLA during a perfunctory conversation some time before, she had spent endless hours at the Berkshire Athenaeum, the town library, poring over the online school catalog. She had decided to study either education or psychology. She wanted a profession that would allow her to interact with and help people. Yet steered by the dynamic winds of fate, for one of her first classes, Lauren found herself in a classroom at 94 Porter Street, the Department of Fine and Performing Arts. Her class, FPA 100, was the passport she needed to continue the journey of finding herself and her place in the world. Curious and a little reluctant, Lauren eventually signed up for THEA 238, Experiencing Performance, and THEA 271, Discovering Plays.

The college's energy and vitality were infectious. She could not help but make such energy her own. In time, Lauren became an honor student and a talented performer within the confines of the MCLA artistic community. She had participated in three school productions by the end of her third semester. The most poignant of the three had been the winter production of *Cymbeline*. Lauren was given the role of Imogen, the heroine, who, despite all odds and multiple attempts to derail her convictions, stays true to her beloved and secret husband, Posthumus.

The first night of the show, Venable Hall was hardly full. Only about fifty people were in the audience, and a quarter of them left before the end of the play. Despite the small turnout, that performance was pivotal for Lauren. During the show, she experienced a strangely muted yet powerful detonation in her soul. Something resonated deep within her while she was bringing to life a fragment of Shakespeare's imagination.

Ere I could
Give him that parting kiss which I had set
Betwixt two charming words, comes in my father,
And like the tyrannous breathing of the north
Shakes all our buds from growing.

In those lines from the first act, Imogen recalls the farewell to her husband, Posthumus, who has just been banished by her father, King Cymbeline. Lauren felt the old fervor of the short-lived but intense affair with Declan. In the end, neither Cloten nor Iachimo, Imogen's suitors, could ever sway her from her husband. It made sense. Lauren could feel Imogen's cemented love for Posthumus as if it were her own.

At the end of the show, as Lauren and her fellow actors took their bows, she saw a kind of joy on the faces of the audience members who had stayed. She realized in that moment, taking in the applause, that she could touch people through what she did on the stage.

Lauren was permeated with a passion for theater that soon became an appendage of her being. Inexplicably, acting also became a type of release for her ever-present emotional ups and downs. Acting allowed her to keep her unyielding love for Declan in perspective. She reached a sort of satisfied resignation to Declan's absence. But whenever a performance called for Lauren to kiss a fellow actor, she always imagined that she was kissing Declan. This seemed to make dealing with her feelings about him easier, and she felt it made her a better performer.

By the time Lauren reached her final semester at MCLA, she was a theater major. Besides her theater classes, she also acquired a robust, well-rounded education in a variety of other subjects, from science to economics. She had soaked up everything her professors taught in every class. Lauren had been an exemplary student, on the dean's list each time.

She had also made new friends—among the faculty too. One of these individuals was Antonious Garelly, the chair of the Department of Fine and Performing Arts. He was well known in the small theater circle in that part of the country. He had been one of the founders of and was still a very influential figure in organizing the region's popular theater festival. Unknown to Lauren at the time, that seemingly small circle, in that provincial area of the country, had ample, prestigious, and a remarkably far-reaching impact in the world of theater.

With her perfect academic record and indisputable talent, professor Garelly found Lauren to be one of the few students whom he felt proud to recommend. One evening, he invited Anabelle Lloyd, a friend and the distinguished director of the prominent Barrington Stage Company, to a fall production of Edward Albee's *Seascape*—Lauren's last performance on campus. Lauren performed the role of Nancy brilliantly, and Anabelle Lloyd loved her on stage. And later, over dinner at Hobson's Choice, she was further captivated with Lauren's enchanting personality.

A few months later, Lauren graduated with a BA in Fine Arts with a theater concentration—and a job.

THIRTY-THREE

Success in any endeavor invariably requires imagination, desire, perseverance, and everlasting competence. But in the fierce realm of theater, even the most gifted performer can occasionally benefit from the serendipitous favor of luck in order to rise above the ordinary.

Lauren was already beyond banality. She could not be happier or more satisfied with how she had molded and re-created herself. She had done so much in just under four years. Even in the midst of that happiness, though, a series of unexpected events catapulted her life into an unforeseen and far-flung dimension.

—∞—

Ray Schoen, Phillip Ankel, and Michael Antin knew it was crunch time. The heads of the Hubert Organization, which owns a number of important theaters on and off Broadway, met for dinner at Bar Americain one spring evening. A deal to bring *Regional Terminal* from London had just fallen through. The successful musical portraying the sardonic lives of two security officers of a small English airport had a cast of twelve. The Hubert group insisted that a production of that size was best fitted to a small theater like the John Golden on Forty-Fifth. Their British counterparts disagreed and argued for a much larger venue. After several months of superfluous meetings in which the bottom-line conflict could not be overcome, the London group finally withdrew. The powerful New Yorkers had never expected nor planned for such an outcome. With *The Avenue* coming to an end after three outstanding years, the trio of corporate heads needed a small but world-class act to keep the seats full at the John Golden Theatre.

Even before Bobby Flay's crab-coconut appetizer with diced mangoes arrived, Michael Antin knew the dinner was more of a potential last supper than an after-hours meeting. The chair of the group, Ray, insisted on ordering for the other two men. After almost unnecessary conversation over pork chops with fig sauce, Michael, the vice president of operations, inherited the responsibility to find a Broadway-worthy production in a few months' time.

Being very good at his job, the VP of operations knew exactly where to look.

—⚏—

Lauren had returned to Pittsfield as an alternate understudy in one of the lead roles of the Barrington's second-stage production of *Fountain*. This meant that she only got to be on stage when both the principal and main understudy actors were unavailable. Lauren never performed her role in *Fountain* with a real audience. As in most hierarchical jobs, there are dues to be paid. She knew this and bowed to her profession's rites of passage.

Not surprisingly, Lauren did not earn very much more than she had two years ago as a waitress. The only difference she could see was that she no longer stood by a table taking orders but rather sat at one and got waited on, whenever she found herself inside the Court Square Café. Of course, there were times when she could not help but offer her friends a hand on a busy day. In addition, she now had more time to enjoy the town's cultural offerings—along with walks and picnics at the Common, and weekend gatherings with friends or her aunt. For the time being, she could not see herself living anywhere else or doing anything else.

Routine, however, is finite.

—⁂—

Cindy Vega's lupus flared with such intensity that she needed to take time off. She had been starring as Christine in the Barrington's main-stage production of A. J. Cronin's modern adaptation of *The Citadel*. Her alternate stepped up to the starring role, and Anabelle Lloyd shifted Lauren as the first understudy. Her character was the wife of a young, idealistic doctor. Lauren already knew all the lines. She had been studying the script on her time off. On one of her frequent visits to the Athenaeum, Lauren had also checked out and read the original novel. She not only identified with but also felt to be exactly like Christine, particularly in her unconditional love for the novel's protagonist, Andrew Manson. She was his guiding light and the motivation that made Andrew tick—as a physician and as a person.

Had she ever been that to her real-life doctor? Did Declan ever feel the void that Andrew Manson experienced without Christine by his side? Did his memory of Lauren ever envelop him with hope or joy and help him, in any way, through a difficult episode in his life over the last four years? Lauren wondered.

—⁂—

As the main understudy, Lauren would play the lead role on stage one weekday and for the matinee on Sundays. Her debut was on a pleasant Thursday evening in late spring. She had secured front mezzanine seats for Robert, Alexis, Jackie, Phil, and a handful of friends. The group, who arrived early to the Union

Street theater, was puzzled by the one reserved seat smack in the middle of their otherwise contiguous seats. If someone was so important, they speculated, why not put them closer to the stage?

"Must be some eccentric, I bet," Robert said.

"Sit on it. Maybe the chair is just broken but all they could find was that sign," joked the usually introverted Phil.

"We'll see," Jackie said with a tone of finality and sat down. Everyone else followed suit.

A short time later, when the theater was nearly full, the lights dimmed. Just as the orchestra began to play, the group of friends was forced to stand as a middle-aged man in a J. Press jacket and bowtie politely murmured his apologies and shuffled sideways toward the empty reserved seat.

The next time they were on their feet, they were clapping enthusiastically as the curtain fell and rose again for the cast's encore bow of thanks. The show had been phenomenal and made even more so by Lauren's formidable performance. Her friends cheered and cried and felt an immense sense of pride to see that the once ordinary but feisty waitress had turned into a splendid actress.

The only person who did not participate in the standing ovation was Michael Antin. Sitting in that previously reserved seat, he simply pumped his fist in concealed excitement and whispered to himself, "I'll save the ovation for New York."

THIRTY-FOUR

Michael Antin insisted on the exact same cast he had witnessed just months before.

The Citadel opened to equally magnificent reviews as those it had garnered in western Massachusetts and Boston. Lauren's name soon became popular in the entertainment section of the *New York Times* and, on several occasions, even on the social pages. She had moved into an elegant studio apartment in Chelsea, not far from Broadway. She never imagined, in her wildest dreams, that one day she would live in a place where doormen greeted her every time she went in and out of her building. She felt fortunate yet humbled by her new environment. Gracious and unperturbed by her amazing new life, Lauren became a favorite in an exclusive society of influential artists and patrons.

In time, she began to indulge in the constant thought that Declan would one day open the *New York Times*, see her name or picture, and rush to New York, from wherever he might be, to see that it was, in fact, that frail girl he once knew and possibly loved. At the very least, she dreamed that he would see her in the newspaper ad and smile—realizing that the troubled girl he once fruitlessly tried to help, had eventually learned from her mistakes. Oh, if he could only see that the same girl had never faltered since, and that she had made something of herself. Lauren always waited a long time after each performance before exiting through the theater's front door, hoping he would be there with a rose in hand and a kiss in mind.

A year went by and he never showed.

— ᴍ —

Declan just did not know.

Once, at the Starbucks on New Haven's Chapel Street, he sat on a chair to sip a latte and fend off a chilly winter breeze. He grabbed loose newspapers left in minor disarray on the end table beside him. One was the entertainment section of the *New York Times*. No sooner had he opened the page where an ad for *The Citadel* occupied almost a quarter of the space than his pager went off. His forearm directly covered Lauren's photo and name as he conversed with the voice on the other end of the line, which beckoned him to make his way to the hospital for a heart transplant. Without another glance at the wide-open section of the newspaper before him, Declan got up and, with latte in hand, left for the hospital. And just like that, unknowingly, he left Lauren behind once again.

— ᴍ —

The momentous and glamorous night on which Lauren won her unanticipated Tony Award was unreal. It marked the culmination of her grit and diligence since receiving a second chance at life. After the ceremony, Lauren looked into the multitude of peering faces behind the temporary blockade on Sixth Avenue. She waved at her friends who had traveled from the Berkshires. Through many more smiles, waves, and photo ops, she kept scanning every face. But Declan was not there.

He will never come, she concluded sadly in her mind.

—⁓—

Despite what should have been one of the happiest moments in her life, Lauren couldn't hide her disappointment. Shrouded in the relative silence of the private black cab on the ride home, she stared at the Tony Award on her lap. It felt empty, not being able to share the trophy—and all that it meant—with the person who mattered most. By the time the cab reached her building, she had already made up her mind: the Tony belonged with Declan. After all, if he hadn't saved her life that fateful night in Galveston, this extraordinary day would never have happened.

Once in her apartment, she looked him up on the internet, wrote down his new work address, and went to bed. The next morning, she went looking for a suitable container and the right card. Later the same day, she mailed the award to Declan, satisfied to know that by sending it, some part of her new self would be with him.

Lauren never expected a response to come back.

—⁓—

But something did come about a week later. It was an institutional envelope from the Yale School of Medicine. Lauren read the letter over and over again. Could it be? Did he know? Who was this person, this *best friend*, anyway? Should she go to New Haven, as the note suggested?

After all, what did she have to lose?

THIRTY-FIVE

Lauren kneeled beside him, locked her arms around his semi-upright body, and cradled his unconscious head against her shoulder. She never thought that the emptiness in her heart could possibly intensify. She lost all senses—the paramedics virtually had to pry her arms open before they could tend to Declan. It was agonizing to the point of madness when the ambulance doors closed and it sped away from her. They would not let her ride with him. She was not family. Lauren could not think fast enough to lie. Still kneeling where Declan had collapsed and with a small crowd around her now, she cried, hoping her tears would carry her from the dark abyss she had plunged into.

It may not have happened were it not for a gentle but steady tap on her shoulder.

"Ma'am. Ma'am?"

She turned to face the young man trying to get her attention and caught a swift glimpse of her old companion.

"Are you with the professor?" the young man asked. In one hand, he held the satchel containing Blossom, who peered through the top opening, and the mahogany box in the other.

"Y-yes." Then, pointing to the satchel and box, she said, "And those are ours."

"Here, he asked me to hold them, but it seems they are better off with you."

"Thank you," Lauren replied as she received Blossom and the box. She hugged the satchel while someone else brought over her jacket and purse, which she had left on the park bench.

With one last fragment of determination still in her, Lauren slowly rose and asked for directions to the hospital.

THIRTY-SIX

W hen I mailed that note to Lauren a couple of weeks prior, I never imagined that my well-intentioned prying would end like that. After the package arrived at my desk that day, out of deep affection for Declan, I thought I could steer the winds of fate just a little. The night I told Frank the story that I had pieced together of the events leading up to Declan's arrival in New Haven, I was hopeful and almost sure that only something good would come of it. I was further reassured that everything would turn out great after I called the Omni Hotel at Yale and verified that Lauren had, in fact, checked in and picked up the package the night before Declan's lecture.

The chief trauma resident called me. After recovering the strength in my knees, inhaling deeply, and regaining my senses, I told the doctor to look out for Lauren and to treat her like family. On my way to the hospital, I called Kate Baltierra and gave her the awful news.

Lauren and Blossom sat in a waiting room outside the operating suites.

My God! She was beautiful—yet modest and genuine. And her love for Declan was achingly evident. I told her I was the one who had sent her the notes; then I sat next to her and carried on a mostly one-sided conversation aimed to soothe us both.

I suggested she get some rest at her hotel or at my house. He would not be out of surgery for a long time, I told her. She politely declined. I took Blossom to my office just across the street and went right back to sit next to Lauren.

The next morning, I collected Kate from the Tweed New Haven Airport. I gave her as factual an update as I could. Then we drove to the hospital mostly in silence. Just before we marched into his room, she grabbed my arm and halted. With a swift glance and a gentle hand gesture, Kate directed my attention toward the partially opened blinds of the window in Declan's ICU room.

There was Lauren, defying all sorts of tubes around him, lying next to Declan, caressing his face, and gently running her fingers through his hair. Kate and I stood there for some time, watching the very picture of love before us.

Finally, we went in behind a nurse who had to administer something through a tube. A kiss and a protracted but affectionate smile between Lauren and Kate led to more silence. There was nothing more to do, nothing else to say. Only time would tell.

—————

Declan remained unconscious. Entrenched within the room, as he had once done for her years before, Lauren talked to him incessantly, hoping he could hear her soothing voice. The nurses allowed her to help him in any way that she wanted, whether it was changing his gowns or placing medication through tubes or adjusting the compressive boots around his calves and a number of other things. Everything she did for him, she did with tenderness and devotion.

Lauren never left his side.

EPILOGUE

Declan eventually left us.

I cried inconsolably in my Frank's loving arms. He could sense my heavy chest but empty heart. Oh, how much I loved Frank. He was never jealous toward the other subjects of my affection—my surgeons, my heroes, and at that time, my Declan. I would miss him dearly.

From a distance, I could not quite meddle in his life anymore. Nonetheless, I kept in touch.

Declan, you see, eventually followed Lauren to New York.

He took a position at Columbia, where he continued to practice surgery and teach at the college in much the same way he had done at Yale. Meanwhile, Lauren's career continued to flourish. She became a household name.

There was no keeping them apart.

—ᴍ—

Weeks after his accident, Declan finally woke up in Lauren's caring arms. He had generated a colossal capacity for love—a love that, with one kiss in the middle of the night, in a marginally disheveled state, in an ordinary hospital room, and with total conviction, he gave in its entirety to Lauren.

They would always be there for each other.

I called them out of guilt one day. I still had their trophy on my desk. I reluctantly asked Lauren if she wanted me to package it and send it back. To my delight, she said no. All she ever wanted, she already had, she told me. We made small talk and then said goodbye. At that very moment, they had been walking down the street, hand in hand, with that funny satchel by their side.

Whenever anyone asks about the trophy on my desk—this former package—I simply tell them, "It's just a long, sweet story and a symbol of true love."

THE END

AUTHOR'S NOTE

I found factual, cultural, and historical information regarding entities and monuments such as El Metro and the Angel of Independence, the legend of Iztaccíhuatl and Popocatépetl, and businesses and institutions mentioned in *The Package* on publicly available websites, including mexonline.com, mexicomaxico. org, metro.cdmx.gob.mx, and Wikipedia.org.

ABOUT THE AUTHOR

RAFAEL SILVA is a graduate of Yale University and the University of Texas Medical Branch at Galveston. He lives in Portland, Oregon, with his wife and their pets.

For fun facts and videos related to THE PACKAGE, visit

limbicpress.com

Made in the USA
Columbia, SC
08 January 2020